Margery Sharp

MISS BIANCA IN THE ORIENT

BERNARD THE BRAVE

Specially produced by MAMMOTH
for SCHOOL BOOK FAIRS LTD

First published in Great Britain as two separate volumes:

Miss Bianca in the Orient
First published 1970 by William Heinemann Ltd
Published 1993 by Mammoth
Text copyright © Margery Sharp 1970
Illustrations copyright © Erik Blegvad 1970

Bernard the Brave
First published 1976 by William Heinemann Ltd
Published 1993 by Mammoth
Text copyright © Margery Sharp 1976
Illustrations copyright © Faith Jaques 1976

This omnibus edition first published 1994 by Mammoth
an imprint of Reed Consumer Books Ltd
Michelin House, 81 Fulham Road, London SW3 6RB
and Auckland, Melbourne, Singapore and Toronto

ISBN 0 7497 1963 X

A CIP catalogue record for this title
is available from the British Library

Printed and bound in Great Britain
by Cox & Wyman Ltd, Reading, Berkshire

Contents

MISS BIANCA IN THE ORIENT

BERNARD THE BRAVE

MISS BIANCA
IN THE
ORIENT

Illustrated by Erik Blegvad

I

THE BANQUET

MISS BIANCA sat before her mirror in the Porcelain Pagoda applying the discreetest possible touch of pomade to her whiskers. (Unusually in a white mouse they were dark brown, like her equally unusual dark-brown eyes.) She had already applied the discreetest possible touch of rose-water behind each ear; she was making a rather special toilet. Her ermine fur, brushed and brushed, shone like silver; her silver necklace, polished and polished, gleamed like dew-drops—or like her beautifully-polished tiny nails. Her tail was practically coiffured. Miss Bianca never looked anything else than extremely elegant, but on this particular occasion she looked quite ravishing!

So certainly thought her dear old friend Bernard, as she emerged to greet him beside the Venetian-glass fountain in the Pagoda's small encircling pleasure-ground. The whole establishment was situated in the schoolroom of an Embassy, which was one reason why Miss Bianca, in addition to her duties as Perpetual Madam President of the Mouse Prisoners' Aid Society, had almost too many social engagements. Bernard, the Society's hard-working Secretary, never went out at all; but if he always came to see Miss Bianca off to a party it wasn't through envy. It was because he admired her so in evening dress.

'What's on tonight?' asked Bernard interestedly.

'Just another banquet,' said Miss Bianca, 'in honour of some newly-accredited Ambassador. I only hope there won't be too many speeches!'

She sighed. She wasn't showing off—Miss Bianca never showed off, she was too well bred—but this was actually her third banquet within a week. The Boy, the Ambassador's son, her patron and playmate, was only just old enough to stay up for them, and badly needed Miss Bianca in his pocket to lend moral support. (To be truthful, Miss Bianca sometimes gave him a gentle nip as well, if he looked like nodding.)

'And to-morrow's the General Meeting,' said Bernard anxiously. 'Do try and get home early, Miss Bianca!'

Miss Bianca sighed again. Since giving up the active rôle of Madam Chairwoman, General Meetings of the M.P.A.S. rather bored her. As Perpetual Madam President, she felt her position too purely decorative. But all the members liked to see her on the platform—the famous

Miss Bianca, leader of how many daring expeditions![1] —
and to hear her famous silvery voice, if only introducing
a speaker. So Miss Bianca always did her duty by a General
Meeting, just as she did by an Ambassadorial banquet,
though she would have much preferred to stay at home
writing poetry. Her first slim volume of verse had gone
into three editions.

Bernard said he'd hang on at the Pagoda anyway, just
to see she got back safely; and with that Miss Bianca ran
off to join the Boy, waiting to put her in his pocket. It
contained already a few salted almonds, so that Miss Bianca
could have a little banquet of her own. She brushed her
whiskers against his thumb in acknowledgement of the
kind thought.

'I do hope you won't find it dreadfully dull, Miss Bianca,'
said the Boy, 'and I do think it's nice of you to come!'

Who could have imagined that this was to be the start
of one of the most perilous adventures even Miss Bianca
had ever undertaken!

2

Actually she found the banquet quite enjoyable. She
had always an eye for the picturesque, and peeping out of
the Boy's pocket was delighted to observe the new
Ambassador, from some Oriental state, attired in cere-
monial robes of Oriental splendour. His cloth-of-gold
and emeralds threw just run-of-the-mill satins and diamonds, and even Orders and other decorations, quite in

[1] A Norwegian poet rescued from the Black Castle, the child Patience from
the Diamond Palace, Mandrake a reformed criminal from the Duchess's
Turret.

the shade! Another piece of picturesqueness was the beautiful letter of credentials he had brought: all the communications that really mattered, between his own and other embassies, were typed, so that carbons could be kept; this particular communication being a purely formal expression of politeness, the Ambassador offered across the dinner-table half-a-dozen lines of Oriental script elegantly brushed on rice-paper and contained in a padded silk pouch embroidered with seed-pearls. Every lady present exclaimed admiringly, and wanted the pouch for a handkerchief-sachet—but of course the Boy's mother, as hostess, had first claim.

'Though the contents must be strictly the property of His Excellency,' smiled the new Ambassador—(all Ambassadors are called Excellencies, to encourage them to be excellent)—'if so gracious a lady cares to accept such a mere trifle as the envelope, my country will be honoured indeed!

The Boy's mother smiled back. She was looking particularly beautiful herself that night, in pale-blue lace and an aquamarine tiara; in fact Miss Bianca strongly suspected that even if she *had*n't been hostess, His Excellency would have found some excuse for giving her that pouch everyone wanted!

'You must permit me to send a little gift in turn, to your Ranee,' said she. (Ranee is the Oriental for queen.) 'Would Her Highness accept, do you think, this trifling thimble?'

For a good Ambassadress, like a good Boy Scout, is always prepared. The thimble the Boy's mother had slipped into her evening bag, (just in case), was gold rimmed with opals—actually a gift from, and fit for, a queen. To be sure it wasn't very practical, because as the

Ambassadress had discovered, any embroidery-silk always tangled on the opals; but it was still extremely pretty and precious—so why should the Oriental Ambassador frown?

'To be truthful, dear lady,' said he, in a lowered voice, (they were naturally sitting next to each other, so a little private conversation was possible), 'Her Highness's requirements in the way of sables, silver foxes and an ermine bedspread ready-made-up absolutely fill all baggage-space on the 'plane that must reluctantly bear me away from you —taking precedence,' he added, frowning again, 'even over sacks of seeds! And if you ask how little weighs even a golden thimble, I can only answer that Her Highness has never employed a thimble in her life; the pouch you so much admire indeed came from the palace, but it was embroidered by one of her ladies . . . In fact,' murmured the Ambassador, lowering his voice still further, 'our highly-ornamental Ranee is one of those anachronisms every new republic has to live with—but I can assure you that in all essentials the Palace and the Capital are worlds apart!'

'How understandable!' murmured the Ambassadress tactfully; then smiled again—smiling, at banquets, being *de rigeuer*. 'Since I mayn't offer a thimble—and you spoke of seeds—what about a packet of mustard-and-cress?'

'Accepted with pleasure!' declared the Oriental Ambassador, now smiling too. So did all the other ladies smile, diplomatically concealing their disappointment; to make up for which the Ambassador was so particularly charming to each in turn, all agreed in the drawing-room afterwards that he had the nicest manners possible!

'And I shall keep his pouch for my very nicest handkerchiefs!' said the Boy's mother.

But the Boy had a different plan. As soon as everyone was gone, he pulled Miss Bianca gently out of his pocket and sat her down on the seed-pearl embroidered square of silk. Has it been mentioned that the silk was pink? It was; Miss Bianca's favourite pale rose-colour. Against it her silvery fur showed up precisely but with extreme delicacy; the biggest pearl was just the right size to fit into the curve of her tail . . .

'Oh, do let's give it to Miss Bianca!' begged the Boy. 'I'm sure she'd like to have it in the Porcelain Pagoda! Just think how cosy she could be, tucked up inside, when it's cold!'

His mother the Ambassadress bent over them affectionately. She had the highest opinion of Miss Bianca, who besides keeping the Boy awake at banquets also sat regularly on his shoulder to help him learn his lessons. It was actually the Ambassadress who had given Miss Bianca her silver chain.

'Why, I really meant to keep such a pretty thing myself,' said she, lightly fingering the beautiful seed-pearl embroidery. 'But as Miss Bianca looks so charming on it, hers it shall be!'

Miss Bianca gracefully bowed her thanks. At the Ambassadress's bidding a footman carefully carried the pouch, Miss Bianca still reclining on it, off to the schoolroom, and set it down inside the Pagoda's pleasure-ground, while the Boy went to bed.

3

'Good gracious me!' exclaimed Bernard—who as will

be remembered was waiting for Miss Bianca's return. 'Whatever's *that*?'

'A gift from the Orient,' explained Miss Bianca complacently. 'Don't you think, my dear Bernard, it will afford a most delightful winter retreat?'

Bernard walked all round the pink silk square admiringly.

'Just the job,' he agreed. 'Either in your boudoir or out here in the grounds. Why, you could sit in it out of doors, and enjoy any sun, all through winter!'

'Exactly what *I* thought,' said Miss Bianca. 'Of course I haven't seen inside yet, but the lining also appears to be of silk, which always promotes comfort. Seed-pearls, inside, I confess I could do without—they're so bumpy!'

'Let's look inside now,' said Bernard eagerly.

He helped Miss Bianca down, and together they raised the embroidered flap. ('Put it up on poles, and you'd have an awning!' suggested Bernard.) Then they pushed apart the silken walls within. These were not pink, but cream, and smelled sweetly of attar-of-roses. A few large needle-holes where the pearls were sewn on afforded perfect ventilation even at the back. There was in fact nothing to mar Miss Bianca's new little nest of comfort and beauty —save that it was occupied already . . .

There in the furthest silk-lined corner lay coiled—a serpent!

ALI

FOR a dreadful moment Bernard and Miss Bianca stood frozen in horror. One thing they both knew about serpents was that some of them eat mice. Then Bernard pounced.—Though never a success in society, lacking the art of easy chit-chat, he possessed other, more valuable qualities. He was wonderfully stout-hearted, and ever prompt in action. The serpent was in fact a very small one; scarcely a snake; rather a snakeling, about four inches long and a pretty green colour, but even had it been a boa-constrictor or python, Bernard in defence of Miss Bianca would have pounced just the same. Not fear, but excitement, made him miss his mark; instead of seizing the intruder by the throat, he landed sitting on its tail.

The serpent, or snakeling, sneezed.

'I suppose you haven't a thermometer?' it asked anxiously. 'I have to watch my temperature; I'm rather delicate.'

All animals speak a universal animal-language, besides their own, so though the accent was strange Bernard and Miss Bianca had no difficulty in understanding, and the homely words did much to calm their fears.

'I have no doubt there is one in the Ambassador's bathroom,' said Miss Bianca. ('Bernard, do get off his tail!) But might one ask—purely as a matter of form—whence and why you are here, also what is your name?'

('I should jolly well think we might!' growled Bernard, without moving.

'How would *you* like a stranger sitting on *your* tail?' rebuked Miss Bianca. Then Bernard moved.)

'Ali,' said the snake, as soon as Bernard's weight was off, gliding out into the pleasure-ground and stretching. 'My name is Ali, and why I'm here I suppose is because I felt a cold coming on. It looked just the place,' he explained, with a wistful backward glance at the padded silken walls, 'to keep away from draughts in . . . So I slipped inside and went to sleep, and when I woke up a whole wad of paper had been pushed under the flap—absolutely *all* draughts excluded!—and I felt so comfy I went to sleep again. But *where* do I wake up?'

'I fear far, far from home,' said Miss Bianca compassionately. 'Your home being doubtless the Orient?'

'Well, of course,' said Ali. 'Isn't *this* the Orient?'

Miss Bianca and Bernard exchanged speaking looks. The country to which the Boy's father was Ambassador was so *un*-oriental, winter lasted six months. On its mountains, snow lay all the year round . . .

'However unwittingly, you have travelled by air,' explained Miss Bianca, 'also I fear to a very different climate.'

'You'll probably freeze to death,' added Bernard hopefully.

Ali sneezed again; then like many persons who have landed themselves in awkward situations, put the blame on someone else.

'It's all that wretched page-boy's fault,' he complained. 'I *thought* he had a cold. Then I thought he was just snivelling as usual, so out of sheer kind-heartedness I let him pick me up and stroke me. Now besides catching it I've been forced to travel (you tell me) by air to a completely unsuitable climate where I shall probably get pneumonia as well. I'd better go to bed at once.'

'Not here you won't,' said Bernard. 'This happens to be a lady's private residence.'

He looked at Miss Bianca eagerly, ready at a twitch of her whiskers to run the intruder out. But Miss Bianca's attention, and though she was by this time quite as disgusted as Bernard by Ali's effrontery, had been preliminarily caught. She was so fond of her own Boy, the mention of any boy whatever always interested her.

'What page-boy?' asked Miss Bianca.

'Why, the Ranee's,' said Ali. ('I suppose you don't mind my just sitting *down*?' he added to Bernard—at the same time making free of one of Miss Bianca's garden-chairs.) 'That is, he *used* to be Her Highness's page; now he's in the elephant-lines waiting to be trampled to smithereens at next full moon—all on account of his snivelling so! Believe it or not, he actually snivelled into Her Highness's sherbet!'

There was a slight pause, while Miss Bianca with her right-hand set of whiskers signalled Bernard to keep quiet and with the left-hand set expressed compassionate emotion.

'If by snivelling you mean crying,' said she, 'why did he cry?'

'Ask me another,' said Ali carelessly. 'Of course he's an orphan: his parents I believe were some sort of medical missionaries, from some quite foreign country, but when *they* died Her Highness was good enough to receive him as a page. She even designed his costume herself—white satin, with a cherry-coloured sash.'

'Enough to console *any* child for the loss of his parents!' agreed Miss Bianca sweetly—but of course meaning the exact opposite. (This is known as irony.) Bernard, more forthright, was about to exclaim that if Ali thought any decent boy could be consoled for anything by having a pink sash tied round his tum then Ali didn't know much about boys; but the latter spoke again first.

'Another thing the little idiot snivelled about was wanting to do lessons,' he recalled. 'Can you imagine anything so ungrateful, when his whole life when he wasn't fetching and carrying was simply a round of pleasure! He *deserved* trampling,' said Ali, 'I suppose you haven't such a thing as a hot-water bottle?'

'No, we haven't!' almost shouted Bernard.

'You needn't be *brutal* about it,' complained Ali. 'I'm not poisonous. In fact I think poison's rather vulgar. I'm perfectly harmless, and all that sort of thing. In fact I'm so particularly sweet-natured, even if you won't give me a bed I shan't hiss a hiss.'

With which he settled himself more comfortably, (in

Miss Bianca's best garden-chair), and went back to sleep again.

2

'Well!' exclaimed Bernard. 'I never thought much of reptiles, but this one takes the cake. Whatever do we do now?'

'Put a rug over him,' said Miss Bianca practically.

'*I*'d turn the fountain on him,' said Bernard.

'Then he probably *would* get pneumonia, and thus become more of a liability than ever,' pointed out Miss Bianca, moving towards the Pagoda, 'whereas after a good, warm night's rest he may awake perfectly fit.'

'Not Ali,' said Bernard. 'If he hasn't a cold he'll have something else. I wouldn't be surprised if he deliberately came out in spots.—Bring *two* rugs, Miss Bianca; one for me as well, because I'm going to keep watch. I'm not going to leave you all alone here with a snake in your grass!'

It was a strange sight indeed that the moon through the schoolroom window shone upon: Ali curled in one garden-chair under one rug alongside Bernard in another under another. But Ali's covering was just a plain sort of blanket-rug, whereas Bernard's was Miss Bianca's own *couvre-pied*, (pale pink silk stuffed with swansdown), off her own *chaise-longue* and smelling deliciously of her own special rose-water. If only Bernard could have felt sure Miss Bianca was going to forget about the Ranee's page, he would have spent the happiest night of his life.

Only of course Miss Bianca, being Miss Bianca, didn't.

3

'In the morning,' meditated Miss Bianca, (combing her whiskers), 'Ali and I must have a really serious talk; for doubtless he will return, as he came, with the Ambassador; and that's only in a couple of days' time, and the full moon at least a fortnight off. Who knows,' thought Miss Bianca, (brushing her tail), 'but that the Ranee is less cruel than Ali presents her—only Orientally thoughtless? A word in season might arouse her better nature; and I'm sure Ali is ideally placed to give it—evidently a familiar of the palace, and I dare say quite a pet! 'Tis true he takes the dreadful affair very lightly,' thought Miss Bianca, (slipping between her pink silk sheets), 'and one could wish he showed a little more backbone; but if one can't appeal to his heart or courage, I'm sure one may to his vanity and self-importance! I'll coach him thoroughly tomorrow,' decided Miss Bianca, (laying head to pillow), 'in some touching little speech, perhaps with actions, and I'm sure I can persuade him!'

Miss Bianca could have persuaded a fox to turn aside from a hen-coop. It was on record in the M.P.A.S. Year-book how she'd once persuaded a cat called Mamelouk not to eat Bernard. She had persuaded even bloodhounds to think of their mothers. She thus (though in all modesty) felt little doubt of being able to persuade Ali to play his part, when it was carefully explained to him next morning.

The only hobble to this sensible plan was that in the morning, Ali wasn't there!

3

IN THE CONSERVATORY

'I'M dreadfully sorry, Miss Bianca,' apologized Bernard, 'but I must have gone to sleep.'

He couldn't understand it. He hadn't even *tried* not to go to sleep—the hours after midnight being just the time when mice are by nature wide awake and on the go. He'd even planned, if he got cramp, to do a little weeding in the Pagoda flower-beds. But Miss Bianca, through her association with the Boy, had come to adopt almost human hours, and Bernard, because he couldn't bear not to associate with Miss Bianca, had unconsciously done the same. So they were both so to speak up late, and it was small

wonder that when Miss Bianca emerged next morning
Bernard had been awake only just long enough to make
a hasty and fruitless search of the grounds and surrounding
schoolroom.

Though small wonder, it was still dreadfully unfortunate. Miss Bianca's expression, upon seeing Ali's chair
empty, and Ali nowhere in view, was such that Bernard
nearly took a header into the Venetian-glass fountain. But
that would have been cowardly, (besides giving Miss
Bianca a lot of bother if there had to be an inquest, and also
he hadn't yet signed the codicil to his will leaving her his
stamp-collection), so he instead made the heartfelt apology
described above, hopefully adding something about good
riddance to bad rubbish.

'Actually I wished to speak to Ali rather particularly,'
said Miss Bianca. 'Have you any idea where he may have
gone?'

'Of course I've looked,' said Bernard, 'and I don't believe he's anywhere in the schoolroom. The trouble is, he's
such a slippery little reptile, I suppose he could have gone
anywhere . . .'

'If he's gone into the Boy's mother's dressing-room,'
said Miss Bianca, 'I'm sorry, Bernard, but I shall never
speak to you again!'

Bernard paled.—The fountain was but a mouse-jump
away; no doubt Miss Bianca could get a doctor's certificate
not to appear at the inquest, and would she really care for
his stamp-collection? As these thoughts rushed through
Bernard's agitated mind—as Miss Bianca turned coldly
away—he nearly did jump.—However at this very moment, most fortunately, the footman bringing Miss
Bianca's breakfast of cream-cheese in a silver bon-bon dish

was heard to observe to the housemaid following with
brush and pan that Thomas Gardener had seen a snake
in the conservatory. 'You don't tell me!' squealed the
housemaid. 'Goodness gracious, I'm glad *I* don't have to
go in there!' 'Only quite a small one,' reassured the footman. 'As one might say, (or rather as Thomas Gardener
says), even ornamental; light green.'

                              2

'So *that*'s where he's got to!' exclaimed Bernard re-
lievedly, as soon as he and Miss Bianca were alone again.
'I suppose one might have expected it—just seeking his
own amusement by slithering off to look at pot-plants!'

'Say rather, seeking his own temperature,' corrected
Miss Bianca. 'Indeed I'm rather heartened by his showing
so much initiative; it gives one better hopes of him. We
must nonetheless rout him out, however, for as I said
before I need to speak to him particularly.'

Her manner remained cold.

It was still so early, Thomas Gardener had gone back
to his own breakfast—far more substantial than Miss
Bianca's: scrambled eggs on bacon topped off by a wing
of cold chicken and a slice of pork pie—and Miss Bianca
and Bernard had the conservatory to themselves. Unlike
the former, who often strolled there with the Boy's
mother, Bernard had never yet set foot within its glazed
doors, and even now scarcely appreciated the floral
treasures spread before him. Surrounded by orchids of
every variety, also camellias in full bloom and trailing
stephanotis, all Bernard wanted to set eyes on was a slim

green tail-tip, (by now possibly spotted), he'd very much like to get his teeth into. Miss Bianca, on the other hand, couldn't help pausing so often in admiration, Bernard began to worry lest Thomas Gardener should return before they'd completed a proper search.—His fears were justified; only those who have looked for a needle in a haystack can estimate the difficulty of looking for a very small green snake in a very large, largely green, conservatory. A hundred dangling tendrils, a hundred exposed roots, might have been Ali, or at least a section of him! Only none, when Bernard impetuously pounced, was, and he'd never apologized to so many vegetables in his life before Miss Bianca's loitering gaze, not his own impatient one, at last detected their quarry.

'Pray cast your eye,' murmured Miss Bianca, 'at the roots of that extraordinarily beautiful *Cattleya cambriensis*!'

Only a tail-tip indeed protruded; yet somehow suggested, by its curve, and immobility, that the owner had slithered in, and coiled himself round, and in the steamy heat, exquisitely canopied by orchids, gone to sleep again . . .

'Ali!' called Miss Bianca, in her most beguiling tones—but quite loudly.

There was no response.

Bernard gave the tail a slight nip. Still no response—except that it retracted, which might have been no more than a physical reaction.

'Oh, dear!' exclaimed Miss Bianca. 'I do hope he hasn't gone into *hibernation*!'

'I shouldn't be surprised,' offered Bernard.

'It's too tiresome for words,' said Miss Bianca, 'when I have so much of importance to discuss with him! Moreover, his Ambassador returns in but two days' time, and how is Ali to travel in a state of complete coma? We must at all costs rouse him!'

'And hold his head under the fountain?' suggested Bernard eagerly.

'At a pinch, even that,' said Miss Bianca, 'and then plenty of black coffee!'

But when they looked again, Ali, for the second time, had totally disappeared. Peering into the hole, which turned out to be quite deep, Bernard couldn't distinguish even the faintest glimmer of the smallest light-green scale . . .

'Let *me* look,' said Miss Bianca.

'No, please don't, Miss Bianca,' said Bernard hastily. 'I dare say, if he overheard, he's feeling pretty bad-tempered; and after all we've only his own word for it that he's non-poisonous . . . It was my fault entirely,' said brave Bernard, 'and anyway it's no use just *looking*; I'll go in after him.'

There was a moment's pause. With mixed emotions, Bernard saw Miss Bianca's whiskers tremble. Why they were mixed was because he hated to see her in any sort of distress, but at the same time felt that despite her dreadful words about never speaking to him again, she still valued him too much to be indifferent to his getting snake-bite.

'I dare say it'll be quite a *mild* sort of poison,' said Bernard, more bravely still.

Lighter than a willow-leaf, Miss Bianca's hand rested upon his arm . . .

'No, Bernard,' said she. 'The risk is too great.'

'No? You really mean no?' almost shouted Bernard.

'The risk is too great,' repeated Miss Bianca. 'Also I

begin to believe him too unreliable,' she added, 'for any useful purpose. Let us leave him to his own selfish devices, and forget him!'

Bernard's heart leapt. He didn't quite understand what she meant about Ali being unreliable, and didn't try to; all he knew was that Miss Bianca and he were friends again, and that was quite enough to make his heart not only leap, but practically somersault. It leapt all the way back to the schoolroom, and if Miss Bianca's manner was slightly preoccupied, Bernard was far too happy to notice.

'Now do please get a good rest this afternoon, Miss Bianca,' said he, as they parted at the Pagoda gate. 'You were up late last night, it's been a trying morning, and there's a M.P.A.S. General Meeting at 1 a.m. Of course you'll be on the platform?'

'Of course!' sighed Miss Bianca.

THE GENERAL MEETING

As has been said earlier, the Perpetual Madam President of the Mouse Prisoners' Aid Society had become rather bored by its General Meetings. She had attended so many! —and save for herself, no one ever seemed to put a motion of any interest! The motions put by Miss Bianca were indeed often interesting to the point of hair-raisingness, for she never let the Society forget its original aim of actually rescuing prisoners, whereas a large body of opinion was in favour of merely cheering them up. Led by Miss Bianca, the Ladies' Guild, the Boy Scouts, even a couple of University professors, had adventured into perils they liked to talk about afterwards, but hadn't at all enjoyed at the time; so it really wasn't surprising if the current mood was rather cautious. Most recent motions dealt with such projects as Meals-on-Wheels for Shut-ins; and of course Shut-ins were in a sense prisoners too; but whoever, delivering a Meal-on-Wheels, (reflected Miss Bianca), had been chased by bloodhounds?

'I must be careful not to set too much store by the picturesque!' Miss Bianca chided herself—and so, as has also been said, made a point of always attending every single General Meeting going.

2

These took place in the Moot-hall, a majestic building which had started life as a claret-cask, and which genera-

tions of mice had fitted out quite beautifully with rows of match-box benches and a platform at one end. The platform itself was carpentered from cigar-box cedar wood, with upon it four walnut-shell chairs, perfect masterpieces of the cabinet-maker's art. Behind hung a richly-framed painting depicting the famous incident of a mouse freeing a lion from a net, alongside a glass case containing the chart drawn by Miss Bianca for use in the expedition to the Black Castle, and several other trophies of the same nature. There probably wasn't another Moot-hall in the world so dignified, commodious and interesting, or so regularly filled full!

Of the four walnut *fauteuils* one was for the present Madam Chairwoman, one was for the Treasurer, one was for Bernard as Secretary, and the last for Miss Bianca as P.M.P. As usual, when Bernard led her on there was loud applause, which Miss Bianca as usual acknowledged with a graceful bow before sitting down to be bored.

'Well, here we all are,' opened Bernard briskly. 'Minutes-to-be-taken-as-read-any-objection-put-your-hand-up . . .'

Not a hand was raised. ('If only someone *would* object!' thought Miss Bianca. 'I'm sure none of them remembers a thing about what was in the last Minutes!') She couldn't put her hand up herself because she *did* remember—Item One, permission granted to hold a teenage dance, Item Two, was there dry-rot in the roof?—and couldn't honestly object to either.

'Fine,' said Bernard. 'I don't think the Treasurer has much to tell us. You most of you seem to be paying your dues all right.'

'A hundred per cent,' agreed the Treasurer.

'So all we've really got on the Agenda,' continued Bernard, 'and especially since there *is*n't dry-rot after all, is the best way of spending 'em; on which point I believe our esteemed Madam Chairwoman has a jolly good idea about extending Meals-on-Wheels to include hamburgers.'

Miss Bianca had often marvelled that Bernard, after sharing every single exotic adventure with her, could still appear so concerned with things like hamburgers. ('Remember the mustard!' added Bernard.) 'Undoubtedly Bernard's is the better nature,' thought Miss Bianca. 'Dear me, I wish I didn't feel so bored!'

'Hamburgers!' exclaimed the Madam Chairwoman, now rising to her feet, also giving Bernard a furious look, for she had meant the hamburgers to come as a surprise.— Miss Bianca sympathized with her, but still felt it rather petty. 'Hamburgers for the house-bound!—what could be more of a treat for the poor dears? And as our Treasurer assures me that there are ample funds for at least a month's experiment, I suppose the really burning question is—'

She paused dramatically.

'Whether they don't get enough mince as it is?' suggested Bernard—suddenly struck by one of his sensible thoughts.

'Not at all,' snapped the Chairwoman, this time without even looking at him. 'It's *onions or not?*'

Immediately quite a hubbub arose from the benches, as one mouse after another jumped up to argue pro or con—some declaring a hamburger without onions to be little more than a whited sepulchre, others pointing out how they'd make all the rest of the food smell, others again relating personal anecdotes of a grandad who couldn't abide onions or a grandmother who practically lived on them. It was all quite exciting in its way—but how *parochial*, thought Miss Bianca! When the whole question was referred to a Committee, and the next item on the Agenda turned out to be merely the decorations for the teenager dance, she felt quite justified in letting her thoughts roam to the Orient . . .

Where a page-boy was sent to the elephant-lines because his tears spoiled a Ranee's sherbet . . .

Where an elephant perhaps but awaited the full moon to trample that page-boy to smithereens!

3

For Miss Bianca, adjuring Bernard to forget Ali, had not intended the plight of the Ranee's unfortunate protégé to be forgotten too. It was indeed the sort of thing Miss Bianca couldn't possibly forget. (To do Bernard justice, if he'd had Miss Bianca's imagination he couldn't have either, but then Bernard had so little imagination at all, the only person he could imagine in distress, without

actually seeing them in it, was Miss Bianca herself. While
she was missing for a whole week in the Diamond Castle
Bernard imagined so feverishly, he wore quite a track
tramping up and down a new wall-to-wall stamp-paper
carpet. At the same time this made him uncommonly
useful in an emergency, because he never suffered from
nerves beforehand.)

'If only Ali hadn't proved such a broken reed!' now
reflected Miss Bianca—quite indifferent, (the teenager
dance rearing its head again), as to whether paper lanterns
would catch fire and the fire-brigade have to be called out.
'He presented so obvious a channel of communication!—
for his Ambassador has certainly too many weightier
matters on his mind to be bothered.'

Miss Bianca naturally knew all about not bothering
Ambassadors. Sometimes when the Boy's father wasn't to
be bothered, even the Boy's mother tiptoed, and once put
off a whole garden-party.

'And I've met no others of his suite at all!' thought Miss
Bianca. 'So who can I possibly contact, visiting the Orient?'

At which moment it suddenly occurred to her that
widely-travelled as she was, she had never visited the
Orient herself . . .

'As for refreshments,' the Chairwoman was saying
firmly, 'the teenagers must provide them themselves.—
Don't you agree, Madam President?'

'Yes, of course; certainly!' said Miss Bianca, returning
to the Agenda with a start. 'I agree with Madam Chairwoman entirely!'

The Chairwoman looked pleased. She was really an
excellent mouse in her way—at least fifteen sons bred up
to take responsible positions in the retail trade, and about

the same number of daughters either respectably married or school-teaching. Grandchildren innumerable came to tea each Sunday after afternoon Sunday-school, and most sang in the choir. She was still pleased to have the famous Miss Bianca's approval!

'And you yourself, Miss Bianca, will I hope present the prize for the best couple in the Viennese Waltz?' she said eagerly. 'I won't inflict the cha-cha on you!'

'I'm so sorry,' murmured Miss Bianca. 'There's nothing I should have enjoyed more than to present prizes for both the waltz *and* (if requested) the cha-cha; only unfortunately I shall be abroad.'

4

'Whatever did you mean by that?' asked Bernard, as he and Miss Bianca stood again at the Pagoda gate. (He always saw her home.)

'Exactly what I said,' replied Miss Bianca. 'I just feel like taking a little holiday abroad. It seems such an opportunity, with the Boy off to summer camp!'

'Whereabouts abroad?' asked Bernard suspiciously.

'Actually the Orient,' said Miss Bianca.

There was a slight pause while Bernard walked in through the gate and pulled up a weed from the nearest flower-bed.—In fact Miss Bianca weeded so carefully herself, what he pulled up wasn't a weed at all, but a pansy resting, and he recognized the error almost at once, but he'd apologized to enough vegetable life already in the conservatory that morning, and wasn't going to start again. He just chucked the pansy-root slap-bang into the middle of Miss Bianca's even more carefully-weeded lawn, careless of how untidy it looked.

'I might have known!' groaned Bernard. 'I suppose it's that wretched page-boy!'

'Wretched indeed!' agreed Miss Bianca—which wasn't quite what Bernard meant. 'What heart could fail to be touched by such a pathetic tale?'

'Well, let's say an elephant's,' rejoined Bernard grimly. 'Oh, Miss Bianca, do pray consider the *size* of an elephant, before you consider tackling one! Haven't you ever heard that even the most ferocious and quite large beasts in the jungle—I dare say hundred-pounders—are afraid of elephants?'

'And have *you* never heard,' countered Miss Bianca sweetly, 'that *elephants* are afraid of *mice?*'

'I have, and I don't believe it,' snapped Bernard. 'In my opinion it's just an old wives' tale.—Speaking of which,' he added, more moderately, 'you do I hope realize that a tale, a word you used yourself first, is probably what the whole thing is, when all you have to go on is the unreliable word of a conceited reptile who probably lifted the whole idea from a movie he saw just to make himself more interesting when he actually caught cold in just some perfectly commonplace way like leaving his galoshes off?'

'I trust you may be right,' smiled Miss Bianca. 'Nothing would give me greater happiness, than to discover your diagnosis, (as it well may prove), perfectly correct. But dear me,' she continued lightly—hoping to stop Bernard looking so desperate by suggesting that all she had in mind was a little air-travel—'how long it is since I've *flown*! Not since I flew to Norway! And how delightfully swift and commodious aeroplanes are, compared with dust-carts

and narrow-gauge railways!' (Miss Bianca, in the course
of prisoner-rescuing, had endured both these uncomfortable modes of transport, so she knew what she was talking
about.) 'Moreover an aeroplane with an Ambassador in it
will doubtless be the swiftest and most commodious type
of all!'

'I see you've got it all taped,' said Bernard.

'Well, naturally,' said Miss Bianca. 'You don't suppose
I could keep my mind fixed on hamburgers—or even teenage dances—for a whole hour? My dear Bernard, I do most
sincerely thank you for your warning; and as I say, I only
hope you're right; but really the whole point is that I *need*
a holiday—and the call of the Orient, combined with air-
travel, is simply irresistible! Peacocks!' exclaimed Miss
Bianca enthusiastically. 'To observe peacocks in their
native haunts, how charming! Possibly I may even stroke
a peacock in its native haunt!' (In fact now that she'd
thought of it, the idea really attracted her.) 'In fact, as the
poet Rudyard Kipling so well remarked,' quoted Miss
Bianca, (at the same time correcting his grammar), ' "*If
you've heard the East a-calling, you will never heed aught
else!*".'

'Then I suppose they'll have to get the Treasurer to
judge the cha-cha,' said Bernard gloomily. 'If it wasn't
you, it was going to be me. When do we start?'

5

Miss Bianca made no attempt to dissuade him from
accompanying her. She felt Bernard was growing too
parochially minded altogether, so that a change would do

him good. She therefore simply thanked him very much, and adjured him to be ready, with hand-luggage only, the following night.

'Since by a most fortunate chance,' explained Miss Bianca, 'the take-off is scheduled for 11 p.m.; under cover of darkness we may slip aboard quite easily.—As to how we *get* to the airport,' she added, (knowing perfectly well what Bernard was going to say next), 'that's easy too: in the Ambassador's, I mean *our* Ambassador's car. He intends to drive to see his colleague off, and with his usual thought-fulness *doesn't* intend, (at that hour of night), to take a chauffeur. We shall have the back part entirely to ourselves.'

POEM BY MISS BIANCA
WRITTEN BEFORE GOING TO BED

O Orient! O magic sound!
O magic name! O magic ground!
Where peacocks and Ranees abound
In colourful profusion!
Or so th' Arabian Nights relate,
And even at this later date
Not I, for one, anticipate
The pangs of disillusion!

M. B.

TO THE ORIENT!

ALL went according to plan. The Ambassador, his eyes fixed on the road, never gave so much as a glance behind him into the back part of the Ambassadorial car: Bernard and Miss Bianca, though they prudently sat on the floor, could have sat on the seat without being noticed! No one noticed them either as they ran between the boots of a sleepy Guard of Honour and then up the gangway into the 'plane itself. All present were too preoccupied by such various duties as exchanging diplomatic compliments, (the two Ambassadors), keeping awake, (the Guard of Honour), and getting airborne on time, (the Captain of the aircraft). If Bernard and Miss Bianca had been the size of poodles, they probably wouldn't have been noticed.

Miss Bianca carried an elegant little overnight bag made of snail-tortoiseshell lined with spider-silk, containing such necessities as a fan, a light chiffon scarf and a flask of eau-de-Cologne. Bernard's galoshes and a packet of cough lozenges—for he had taken warning from Ali's sneezes—were tied up in a spotted handkerchief. Miss Bianca had often urged him to buy a proper brief-case, as more befitting his position as Secretary to the M.P.A.S., but Bernard was absolutely devoted to his spotted handkerchief ever since Miss Bianca once jumped down into it as into a safety-net, and so probably saved her neck, in the Black Castle. Though touched to see it still in use, the latter was none the less glad they hadn't to take provisions, be-

cause Bernard's spotted handkerchief with a few sardine-
tails sticking out would really have looked quite dis-
reputable!—Bernard had seen her point in a way, and
suggested taking something more refined and less oily,
like toast-crumbs; as he pointed out, cough-lozenges were
more medicine than grub. But Miss Bianca wouldn't hear
even of toast-crumbs: having often flown before, she
knew that in every passenger-'plane there is a beautiful
young lady dispensing delicious food, sound advice, light
literature, general information, and anything else needed.
These models of female perfection are called Air Hostesses;
and it was under the protection of an Air Hostess that Miss
Bianca intended she and Bernard should travel. Miss Bianca,
besides all her other qualities, had the top executive's gift
of delegating responsibility whenever possible.

Thus no sooner was the 'plane airborne than the Hostess,
taking off her cap before the mirror in her own private
cubicle, beheld two mice seated on the shelf underneath
each wearing a label inscribed 'GIFT TO THE RANEE.'

The labels themselves were visiting-cards which Miss
Bianca had thoughtfully borrowed from the Ambassador.
Hers was attached to her silver chain, Bernard's just tied
round his neck with a bootlace.

'Good gracious me!' exclaimed the Air Hostess. (She
didn't scream, as some ladies do at the sight of mice. Air
Hostesses never scream. Even at the sight of baboons loose
in the luggage-rack an Air Hostess remains calm.) 'Good
gracious me!' repeated the Air Hostess, as she finished
reading. 'How did you get out of your cage?—Or travelling compartment,' she added, meeting Miss Bianca's
slightly reproving eye. (Air Hostesses are noted for their
sensitivity and tact.) 'Obviously you are V.I.P.s indeed,'

she continued, 'but what on earth am I to do with you?'

Since they weren't on earth, but in the air, Miss Bianca just sat back and again delegated responsibility. Bernard, who already admired the Air Hostess extremely, with equal confidence sat back and smoothed his whiskers. (Bernard's whiskers haven't so far been done justice to: though short, they were remarkably strong.)

'At any rate I must declare you to the Captain!' decided the Air Hostess.

So she carried Bernard and Miss Bianca off on a soap-dish to the Captain's cabin.

'Presents for the Ranee?' said the Captain. 'Why, we must have a hundredweight of stuff for her already! Just see they go with the rest, Miss Fitzpatrick—and you might drop a word to the passengers about what fun monsoons are . . .'

Thus Bernard and Miss Bianca travelled airborne to the Orient in the most comfortable conditions imaginable. Miss Bianca slept on the Hostess's own cushion, Bernard in her box of Kleenex. Their meals were scrumptious—green salad, coffee-cake, and three kinds of cheese. In fact they were quite sorry, at least Bernard was, when the time came to disembark; in fact Bernard was so busy saying good-bye to the Hostess, it was left to Miss Bianca to appreciate the skill with which the Captain made a perfect three-point landing on an air-strip scarcely wider than his 'plane's wing-span.

'How hazardous, yet how elegant!' thought Miss Bianca —for scarcely two furlongs beyond where the propellers stopped whirling rose the blank wall of a marble palace— the very last sort of thing an aircraft would want to over-run into! Actually this happened to be the only level area

in the whole of the mountainy Republic the Oriental
Ambassador represented, and actually the strip was already
being widened: as she paused on the gangway Miss Bianca
observed the enormous shape of an elephant trampling
smooth an equal breadth adjoining . . .

'My first elephant!' breathed Miss Bianca rapturously.
In the evening light its shadow stretched for yards and
yards—to a mouse it was like contemplating one's first
Alp! 'Let me imprint the image on my memory for ever,'
thought Miss Bianca, 'so that I may one day write a poem
—nay, an epic!—on the subject!'

She couldn't linger imprinting, however, because at
that moment the Air Hostess, with Bernard in one hand
already, picked her up in the other. On the air-strip two
cars awaited: the Ambassador, followed by his suite,
immediately got into the first and it immediately drove
off, while the second was as immediately loaded with bales
and parcels all addressed to Her Highness the Ranee, and
of course Bernard and Miss Bianca, with their labels round
their necks, were put in too. But theirs didn't follow the
Ambassador's car, for while he was bound to make his
report in the capital hundreds of miles off, the car bearing
gifts for the Ranee had but to circle her palace's marble
walls to the entrance on the other side. The capital and the
palace were worlds apart indeed!

They were also worlds apart *mechanically*. While the
Ambassador's car rolled smoothly and rapidly away, that
containing Bernard and Miss Bianca ran out of petrol at
once.—Its chauffeur, an empty can in hand, strolled back
to beg from the aircraft: Miss Bianca, to whom all in-
efficiency was anathema, shifted impatiently on whatever
it was she was sitting on. It wasn't at all comfortable—thin

and crackly at one end, bumpy at the other; on closer
inspection, it turned out to be a packet of mustard-and-
cress . . .

A point Miss Bianca had often before noticed about air
travel was that however swiftly one travelled *in* the air,
there were absolutely no places like air terminals for
general hanging about. As the discussion between the
chauffeur and the Captain of the aircraft opened, continued, and looked likely to continue, Miss Bianca
preferred action of any kind to bored passivity.—A paper
packet of mustard-and-cress weighed scarcely heavier
than her overnight bag; while Bernard was still straining
for a last glimpse of the Hostess, out ran Miss Bianca,
pulling the packet after her, and with nimble feet sowed
its contents just in front of the propellers and was back in
the car long ere the necessary petrol was being poured into
its tank.

Then they were off at last and at last achieved the short
distance to a gateway second in marble beauty only to the
Taj Mahal.

2

'One bale of sables,' checked the chauffeur with the
door-keeper, 'two of silver fox, one ermine bedspread
ready-made-up, also a couple of mice—though where
they've got to I don't know!'

Actually Bernard and Miss Bianca were inside the palace
already with their labels off. The latter was so used to having the *entrée* everywhere, she easily ignored even so
magnificent a specimen of a door-keeper as the Ranee's.

(Almost seven feet high, in scarlet with gold epaulettes and a scarlet-and-gold turban.) It was Bernard who said shouldn't they tip him; Miss Bianca ignored the suggestion too and walked straight in—Bernard naturally following —and while the baggage was still unloading both had gained the entrance-hall.

'Bless my whiskers!' marvelled Bernard.

The hall was indeed quite spectacular. Its walls were faced with pale pink marble, and the twelve pillars supporting a dome above a fish-pool alternately of jasper and porphyry. The pool itself was tiled with lapis-lazuli, against which the scales of a few fat lolling carp gleamed topaz-bright. Miss Bianca was struck to admiration herself; even though she felt the whole *décor* rather too technicolour to be in perfectly good taste, standards of taste varied, thought Miss Bianca, from clime to clime—and hadn't she expected the Orient to be colourful?

Bernard for his part experienced chiefly a sort of overcomeness, as after eating too many marsh mallows, but bravely tried not to show it.

'Where do we go from here?' he asked—as if '*here*' was just a familiar bus-stop, or suburban railway station, instead of being all over pink marble. 'I mean, what do we do next?'

'Present ourselves to the Ranee, of course,' said Miss Bianca briskly. 'But first we should be properly dressed!'

Extracting the chiffon scarf from her overnight bag, she rapidly tied it over her nose and in a bow behind.

'As a yashmak,' she explained to the goggling Bernard. 'A yashmak, or veil, such as is worn by all ladies in the Orient. I hope you find it becoming?'

'No,' said Bernard. 'I'm sorry, but I don't, Miss Bianca.

I can't see your whiskers.'

''Tis still ever wiser to conform to custom,' said Miss Bianca. '*You* must wear a turban!'

With equal swiftness and decision she seized Bernard's spotted handkerchief—(he'd accidentally left his galoshes and cough-lozenges behind in the aeroplane)—and wound it round his ears.

—It must be acknowledged that whereas Miss Bianca

in a yashmak looked quite fascinating, Bernard in a turban
looked rather silly. Peering at his reflection in the pool, he
felt he'd never looked sillier, even when disguised as a
member of the M.P.A.S. Ladies' Guild. Still brave
Bernard did not flinch; and it is even braver to be brave
while looking silly than to be brave while looking not.

'Lead on!' said Bernard gamely.

Miss Bianca did so. Besides being used to having the
entrée, she was so used to being in places like palaces and
courts and embassies and so on, she had little difficulty in
guiding their steps through corridors of ever-increasing
splendour—first plain marble, then marble inlaid with
scraps of looking-glass, then marble inlaid with topaz—
until through an arch inlaid with turquoise they reached
the Ranee's private apartment. Here the walls were inlaid
with jade; underfoot, for what seemed like miles, stretched
a wonderful silk carpet woven all round the border with
a pattern of pomegranates and in the middle with a great
peacock. Beyond, upon a dais, glittered a low divan heaped
with cushions covered in silver brocade. Somehow sus-
pended before it a row of jewel-like humming-birds,
though stuffed, appeared to quiver in the air, their tiny
claws upholding a panel of finest gauze as a kindly pre-
ventive against anyone being blinded by the Ranee's
beauty as there she sat on her silver brocade cushions
surrounded by a dozen or so ladies sitting lower down.

'My whiskers!' muttered Bernard again. .

Miss Bianca, though silently, agreed with him. The
Ranee was in fact the most beautiful person either of them
had ever beheld.—Most Ambassadors' wives, of whom
Miss Bianca had seen scores, are good-looking; the Boy's
mother was quite lovely; but not one could hold a candle

to the Ranee. Her face was a perfect oval, her complexion ivory lightly flushed with rose; beneath eyebrows black and graceful as a swallow's wings lashes even longer than Miss Bianca's shaded a pair of glorious dark eyes. As for her mouth, it was so rose-like in colour and petal-shapeliness, one almost imagined it a rose indeed, only with for heart a glimpse of pearl . . .

Besides being so beautiful, she was also exquisitely dressed. Over trousers of some light Oriental gauze—dark blue, embroidered with sapphires—she wore by way of contrast a white silk tunic barely touched with silver. Her jewels were equally well-chosen and becoming: a diamond necklace fastened with a sapphire clasp, about twenty-four diamond bracelets, and in her wonderful dark hair six or seven diamond stars.

'*She* isn't wearing a veil,' muttered Bernard.

'Because we are in her private apartments,' murmured Miss Bianca, swiftly removing her own yashmak, and indeed feeling happier as her whiskers sprang out again. 'But do you keep your turban on, Bernard; it looks more respectful.'

At which moment, the Ranee yawned. All the ladies sitting round her looked nervous. One hastily offered a little gold dish of crystallized violets, another a little gold dish of pistachio nuts. The Ranee nibbled a nibble from each with her pearly teeth, then yawned again.

'Now is our time!' whispered Miss Bianca. 'Evidently conversation flags; I don't think we shall be unwelcome!'

Bernard following, she advanced boldly over the peacock-carpet to within a foot of the cushion-throne. There she halted and bowed, while Bernard took three paces forward, then one back, and pulled his whiskers.

There was indeed no doubt of their welcome!

'Good gracious!' exclaimed the Ranee delightedly. 'Fill someone's mouth with gold! See, just as I'm about to expire from boredom, someone's found me two nice new pets!'

3

It was a moment that called for all Miss Bianca's diplomacy, self-forgetfulness in a good cause, general sharp-wittedness and *savoir-faire*. Both she and Bernard strongly objected to being called pets—Miss Bianca could positively feel Bernard beginning to bristle—but at the same time she immediately perceived that to introduce herself as Perpetual Madam President of the M.P.A.S. would cut no ice with the Ranee. In the latter's glorious dark eyes Miss Bianca instantly and accurately read merely a desire to be entertained before she expired of boredom, and absolutely no interest whatever in even such things as Meals-on-Wheels.

'That is, I suppose they can *do* something?' added the Ranee—already impatient! 'They can dance or sing or something?'

'You can jolly well suppose again!' muttered Bernard furiously. 'The lady I have the honour to escort—'

'Hush!' adjured Miss Bianca. 'Is this a time for *amour propre*? Impersonate a wandering minstrel!'

For her eye had been most fortunately caught by a little bibelot in the shape of a miniature harp standing on a low mother-of-pearl table beside the Ranee's cushion-throne. Miss Bianca instantly ran up and struck a few chords. The strings, though of gold wire, responded sweetly to her touch; even though each pedal was a pearl, and thus dreadfully slippery, she managed to control them. First she played 'Greensleeves', then that exquisite mouse minuet *Le Camembert*, while Bernard, without knowing it—he'd just rushed up to be at her side—appeared by his agitated gestures to be turning over invisible music for her. The effect upon the Ranee was instantaneous.

'It's the prettiest thing ever seen!' declared the Ranee.

'The prettiest thing ever seen!' echoed all her ladies.

'I shall take both into my service at once!' decided the Ranee.

'Her Highness will take both into her service at once!' all the ladies told each other.

'Prepare everything mice like to eat, also a suitable cage!' ordered the Ranee.

All the ladies rushed out, leaving Bernard and Miss Bianca alone to amuse Her Highness.

It proved no light task. The Ranee was so enchanted by Miss Bianca's touch in *Le Camembert*, she demanded it

again and again, until Bernard saw Miss Bianca so fatigued, he had to fan her with his whiskers. This enchanted the Ranee even more—('Prepare a cage of gold!' cried she, to her returning ladies)—and Bernard no less than Miss Bianca was quite exhausted before the Ranee remembered three hundred guests to dinner.

'But you shall entertain me again to-morrow!' she promised. 'To-morrow, you shall entertain me all day long!'

4

The golden cage produced by the Ranee's ladies was as commodious as splendid, having once housed a pair of cockatoos. (A long scarlet tail-feather, still dangling between the bars, added further splendour.) Bernard moved into a little upstairs flat, originally a bird-seed pan, while Miss Bianca took the ground floor. The eager ladies supplied bedding out of their own pockets—that is, out of their own pocket-handkerchiefs—and two of the youngest and prettiest brought in addition to cream cheese and crystallized violets a scent-spray containing attar of roses to spray all about and make it smell nice.

'Well!' said Bernard, as soon as they were gone. 'I can't say I much liked being taken for a wandering minstrel, but these quarters are absolutely A.1!'

'Nothing could be more comfortable,' agreed Miss Bianca. 'And really, my dear Bernard, I'd no idea you had such a talent for amateur dramatics!'

This was particularly tactful, as making him feel rather pleased with himself, instead of that he'd made rather an ass of himself. But indeed Bernard seemed in an unexpectedly good mood altogether. For one thing, he didn't even bristle about the cage being a cage—as a rule, being in anything like a cage made Bernard bristle at once!—and even suggested thinking up a name for it, like the Porcelain Pagoda.

'Like "Home Sweet Home",' offered Bernard.

'Why not "*Chez* Cockatoo"?' smiled Miss Bianca. 'Now I can't keep my eyes open a moment longer!' she added. ''Tis high time to say good-night!'

Bernard of course made for his upstairs flat at once.— On its threshold he paused.

'I say, Miss Bianca!' he called down.

'Well?' yawned Miss Bianca, already slipping between sweet-scented handkerchief-sheets.

'Possibly you didn't notice,' said Bernard, 'but *I* did: in the whole of the Ranee's court there wasn't a single page-boy to be seen! She doesn't *have* page-boys! Good-night, Miss Bianca.'

6

AT THE COURT OF THE RANEE

'DEAR ME!' thought Miss Bianca, as soon as she woke next morning. 'What Bernard says is correct: there *weren't* any pages!'

Sitting up and considering, she distinctly remembered the Ranee's constant crunching of nuts or crystallized violets during the pianissimo movement of *Le Camembert*, also that each little golden dish was offered by one of her ladies. On the other hand, if there hadn't been any page-boys, there hadn't been any sherbet either.

'Perhaps 'tis only sherbet the pages serve?' meditated Miss Bianca. 'By some Oriental custom? Today let me watch carefully!'

2

She had ample opportunity to do so, since the Ranee was so delighted with her new pets, she kept them beside her at every waking hour. (It may be said at once, in case anyone besides Bernard is worried over Miss Bianca becoming thoroughly exhausted, that this crush didn't last long; quite soon Miss Bianca was summoned to the harp only at evening.) During that first next day, however, she was constantly at the throne-side; and had ample opportunity to observe the sherbet-service that went on all morning each hour on the hour—but performed strictly

by Her Highness's ladies. Cups of coffee also appeared, and trays of Turkish Delight—the Ranee was always either sipping or nibbling something—but never a sign of a page-boy.

'Strange!' thought Miss Bianca. 'Can it be that the unfortunate orphan described by Ali was Her Highness's single and solitary experiment in that direction, never repeated? Or has Bernard been correct all along, in his suspicions of Ali's utter if imaginative untrustworthiness?'

She honourably relayed these thoughts to Bernard himself. Though naturally pleased, he was too big—just as Miss Bianca was too big *not* to relay them—to say anything like 'I told you so', but instead listened sympathetically when she went on to think (aloud) that a few discreet enquiries were still called for.

'Though if you're going to enquire of the Ranee,' said Bernard dubiously, 'whether she had a youngster sent to the elephant-lines just because he snivelled a bit—'

'I agree 'twould be hardly tactful,' said Miss Bianca. 'I believe I'll ask Willow . . .'

3

Willow was the oldest of the Ranee's ladies: willow-slim indeed, also quivering, like a willow, with sensibility. Striking the harp, Miss Bianca had observed Willow's face through the strings fixed in a look of such sweet, sad rapture, she'd have played for her alone!—But it was also a *sensible* face, and Miss Bianca, ever famous for her swift summing-up of character, at once felt Willow her best source of information. Unluckily, however, there never seemed an opportunity to broach the subject, for the latter, whenever not on duty in the throne-room, had a knack of disappearing. Miss Bianca truly regretted it, though when she learnt the reason, during a talk with the very youngest and prettiest lady, (the one who'd sprayed *Chez* Cockatoo with scent, and whose name was Vanilla), she thought more highly of Willow still.

'Darling Willow takes such care of us all, she never has a *moment*,' explained Vanilla. 'Some of us come into Her Highness's service so young, and miss our families so, we sometimes cry in bed a little—don't we, Muslin?'

Muslin was the second prettiest of the Ranee's ladies, and the one who'd brought the cream cheese and crystallized violets.

'And then darling Willow comes and holds our hands,' continued Vanilla, 'and if you want she'll teach you to embroider, or dance, or sing, or even play chess—all sorts of things!—and takes such pains, she never has a spare moment!'

'Good Willow!' reflected Miss Bianca. 'Is it not just what one might have expected, from your sensitive, sensible and charming countenance? One can well imagine you never have a spare moment! And am I come to add to your pains and agitate you with my distressing enquiries?—Perhaps I needn't after all,' thought Miss Bianca suddenly, 'for I certainly don't mind agitating Muslin and Vanilla!'

The three were chatting outside *Chez* Cockatoo— Muslin and Vanilla having taken it upon themselves always to see Miss Bianca back to bed after a concert.

'And how long have *you* been at the palace, my dears?' asked Miss Bianca interestedly.

'Oh ages!' said Vanilla.

'Years and years!' said Muslin.

'So that if within the last *month*,' continued Miss Bianca, 'there had been any page-boy in the Ranee's service, and if he had been sufficiently unhappy as to cry into Her Highness's sherbet, and as a consequence be sent to the elephant-lines, you'd remember?'

Both Muslin and Vanilla looked quite horrified!

'How could we? No one's *ever* unhappy in Her Highness's service!' declared Vanilla. 'It's a rule—isn't it, Muslin?'

'The first rule,' agreed Muslin.

'But one which a lonely little boy might find difficulty in learning?' suggested Miss Bianca.

'Only there never *was* such a boy,' declared Vanilla

positively. 'Can *you* remember any page-boy crying into Her Highness's sherbet, Muslin?'

'Never!' shuddered Muslin.

'You're quite certain?' pressed Miss Bianca.

'Quite, quite certain!' declared Muslin and Vanilla with one voice.

'Good gracious,' Miss Bianca told herself, 'I believe I really *am* going to have a holiday!'

According to Bernard, (better pleased than ever at Miss Bianca's fresh report), more than a full week of holidaying lay ahead; for Bernard had taken a look at the Air Hostess's time-sheet—he was afraid she might be overworked—and could confidently affirm that the 'plane's next take-off westwards, again with the Ambassador on board, wasn't scheduled before nine days' time.

4

Certainly there was no better place for holidaying than in the Ranee's palace. The way the day went was like this:

First, until the Ranee woke, which was usually late, all was as still and silent and restful as a lily-pool. Of course all the ladies were awake earlier, but moved about on tip-toe, and sipped their coffee, and helped each other arrange their hair and jewels and saris, with no more rustle than the first breath of a dawn breeze. This was a period Miss Bianca particularly enjoyed. Slipping out from *Chez Cockatoo* to watch, she felt she'd never witnessed anything prettier than Her Highness's ladies tip-toeing about, and arranging each other's saris and jewels and hair, all as 'twere in a silent film!

Then as soon as Her Highness woke up a silver bell summoned them to Her Highness's private marble bath, to lave her in rose-water, and then dry her on swansdown towels, before perfuming her with musk and amber and essence of jasmine. Her own morning coffee was floated to her on a little tray of cedar wood carved in the shape of a lily-pad.

After which exertions the Ranee adjourned to her divan-throne, (now spread with an ermine bedspread ready-made-up), to partake of the light refreshments already described until lunch-time, and after lunch went to sleep again, while the ladies adjourned to their swimming-pool, where the scene was far livelier. They splashed each other, sometimes even ducked each other, threw gaily-coloured balls to one another, often shrieking with laughter—for during this period the Ranee was by her own command counted only semi-asleep, and rather enjoyed, since it was her declared aim to make everyone about her happy, sounds of (distant) merriment.

Then when Her Highness had sufficiently roused to take tea the next two hours were spent in bathing and dressing her afresh before she re-ascended her throne to be entertained before she died of boredom.

Miss Bianca was truly shocked at the amount of entertainment needed to prevent this happening. 'To be so rich, and lovely, and yet so bored!' thought Miss Bianca distressfully. 'No doubt 'tis a fault of education; but how unfortunate the result! I wonder if I could interest her in Meals-on-Wheels?'

But even Miss Bianca, who always tried to take the best view of human nature, felt probably not. The Ranee's glorious dark eyes lit with some spark of interest only at

the sight of jugglers juggling, or acrobats somersaulting,
or when Miss Bianca played upon the harp or when one
of the numerous court poets recited a poem in praise of
her beauty . . .

To Miss Bianca this last phase of each evening's entertainment was by far the most enjoyable. Though the
subject-matter was necessarily rather monotonous, as a
poet herself she was always interested in technique. Poetry
written in Oriental, discovered Miss Bianca, had very short
lines, with the same few number of syllables in each, and
no more than six lines altogether making up a stanza. Miss
Bianca quite marvelled at a poet's skill in comparing the
Ranee to a lotus, a gazelle and the full moon all so to speak
in a single breath!—and soon determined to try her hand
herself, though upon a different theme.

POEM BY MISS BIANCA
WRITTEN IN ORIENTAL

Bulbuls[1] in groves
  Stretch forth their throat:
Mingling with doves'
  Musical notes
Sweet to the ears
  Of boatmen in boats.

M. B.

As a first attempt it was really excellent—only one
syllable too many in the last line. 'But how lacking in
heart!' thought Miss Bianca; and to be true to her own
muse, immediately sought inspiration afresh.

[1] Oriental for nightingale.

POEM BY MISS BIANCA WRITTEN
WITH MORE INSPIRATION

Far, far have we flown, o'er mountains and foam,
O'er deltas and deserts, brave Bernard and I!
Shall we e'er feel again the kiss of the rain
Or watch for the first fall of snow?
Ah, no, I much fear me, ah no!

'But this is perfectly ridiculous!' Miss Bianca admonished herself. 'Of course we shall—and Bernard will be complaining about how his chimney smokes, and I sealing the double windows in my Pagoda!'

So she hastily composed two lines more.

Of course we shall!—and well content
Discuss our venture to the Orient!

M. B.

Bernard liked this second poem very much. The first he frankly admitted he couldn't make tail or whiskers of— especially since bulbuls sounded to him like some sort of peppermint; and even after Miss Bianca had explained, wouldn't boatmen in *boats*, pointed out Bernard, presumably fishing, be too far offshore anyway to hear either doves *or* nightingales? But the second poem, with brave Bernard in it, he liked so much he learnt it off by heart.

Miss Bianca's chief allies at the Ranee's court continued to be Muslin and Vanilla. They were best friends. Muslin was dark, Vanilla fair, but owing to their common expression of sweetness and good nature, looked rather alike. They proved indeed the best-natured girls imaginable, and did everything in their power to make Miss Bianca happy.

'Because we've quite fallen in love with you!—haven't we, Muslin?' cooed Vanilla.

'Because we think you're the sweetest and cleverest little thing we've ever seen—don't we, Vanilla?' cooed Muslin.

If there was something rather schoolgirlish about their devotion, Miss Bianca only smiled. The affectionate pair indeed took as much care of her as possible—Muslin always ready to carry her to bed after an over-long session at the harp, Vanilla, (the bolder spirit), always ready to chaperon a run for fresh air on a door-sill. Miss Bianca in turn grew truly fond of the two friends, and truly appreciated their company—especially after Bernard left *Chez* Cockatoo to take up quarters in the stables.

It wasn't exactly Bernard's fault that he became *persona non grata*—which translated from diplomatic means about as welcome as a gumboil—in the Ranee's throne-room. It just so happened that while Miss Bianca was giving her third or fourth recital on the harp, and while Bernard was pretending to turn over music for her, he sneezed. The air of the throne-room was so thick with scent, (and Bernard didn't even smoke), a whiff of musk caught him unawares. Luckless Bernard sneezed and sneezed; the Ranee frowned and frowned; and Miss Bianca thoroughly agreed with her new friends that he had better make himself, at least temporarily, scarce.

'No one would notice him in the stables,' said Vanilla kindly. 'I believe they're quite full of common brown mice!'

Naturally Bernard disliked being taken for common

almost as much as he disliked being taken for a pet or a
wandering minstrel, and Miss Bianca sympathized with
him; but she couldn't help feeling a change of address
sensible. As she pointed out, he could still keep on his flat
at *Chez* Cockatoo and drop in from time to time.

'But what about *you*, Miss Bianca?' argued Bernard.
'How can I possibly leave you all alone and unprotected
at night?'

'I dare say Muslin and Vanilla will accommodate *Chez*
Cockatoo in their sleeping apartment,' smiled Miss Bianca.

'Indeed we will!' cried Muslin and Vanilla. 'There's just
the proper space between our beds!'

Faced by three females, all of them beauties, Bernard
knew he hadn't a chance; and shifted quarters within the
hour.

5

Actually Bernard was a great success in the stables. As a

rule, when out on expedition with Miss Bianca, he was so anxious for her safety every minute he could never take an opportunity to enjoy himself even if one offered; but seeing her so obviously cherished and protected he for once felt free to get around a bit, and chummed up with a set of bachelor mice who taught him to play polo.—The gear was neat, if old-fashioned, pith-helmets, and Bernard easily borrowed one, in which he felt far more at home than in a turban. As he for the first time took the field he in fact looked rather dashing, and only wished Miss Bianca there to see.

Those who have never played polo, (as of course Bernard hitherto hadn't), cannot conceive with what force the opposing ponies and their riders rush down upon each other. Bernard, clinging to the root of his pony's tail, (Number Three), had the breath almost knocked out of his body. Rough words equally beat about his ears as a princely rider reined and checked.—Bernard didn't know what else to do, so he nipped as hard as he could on a shining quarter and found himself carried, with acclaim, through the opposing goal . . .

After so successful a *début* Bernard played polo regularly. His team was called the Princely Orchids. He was also put up for, and joined, the Mouse Oriental Polo Club.

So Bernard was having a holiday too—while as for Miss Bianca's own success at court, it was quite spectacular!

7

AN UNWELCOME GIFT, AND
WORSE TO FOLLOW

'See what the Ranee's given you!' cried Vanilla, opening her handkerchief.

'Look what the Ranee's given you!' echoed Muslin.

Miss Bianca gasped as out tumbled a ruby necklace, two pairs of diamond ear-rings, and several diamond or emerald rings. (They were actually just what the Ranee had lying about on her dressing-table. Its drawers contained ten times as much in the way of jewellery. Her strong-box contained an opal the size of a peach and pearls bigger than pigeons' eggs.) It was still an immensely valuable gift, and as Vanilla pointed out, more valuable still as a mark of the Ranee's favour.

'I'm really overwhelmed!' said Miss Bianca.—The next moment she was indeed; as Muslin looped the rubies about her neck, Miss Bianca sat down with less than her usual grace. 'Let's try twining them round your tail,' suggested Vanilla anxiously, 'for you really and positively must *wear* them, darling Miss Bianca!' But with her tail wreathed in rubies Miss Bianca was simply anchored. 'If you'd let us ever so gently pierce your ears,' suggested Muslin, 'I'm sure you could wear at least the ear-rings!' 'I'm sorry, but I'm quite sure I couldn't,' said Miss Bianca firmly. 'Why, I should feel as though I were wearing a *yoke*!' (There was a double meaning in this which neither of the ladies appreciated.) 'In fact,' said Miss Bianca, 'grateful as I am to Her

Highness—if necessary I'll make a song about it—such a mass of jewellery is really too much for me to support.'

Even if she could have she wouldn't have, because she considered any *mass* of jewellery extremely vulgar. Naturally Miss Bianca couldn't say this to Muslin and Vanilla, who wore every trinket they possessed from the moment they got up.

She saw them look at each other in dismay.

'Dear, darling Miss Bianca,' said Vanilla earnestly, 'you really and positively must wear at least *part* of the Ranee's gift about your person, or she'll be quite terribly offended —and not only with *you*, with *us*!'

The last thing Miss Bianca wanted was to get the pair into trouble.—One of the emerald rings, though the stone was superb beyond belief, had for shank but a slim hoop of gold; and after trying it on Miss Bianca found she could

wear it round her neck without actual discomfort, much
to the relief of her two friends.

'You must still make up that song, Miss Bianca!'
warned Muslin.

SONG COMPOSED BY MISS BIANCA TO EXPLAIN
WHY SHE WASN'T WEARING A RUBY NECKLACE
AND DIAMOND EAR-RINGS ETC. AS WELL

O'ercome with gratitude I sing,
                  (warbled Miss Bianca to the harp)
The humble wearer of Her Highness' em'rald ring!
Rubies and diamonds too? Ah, far too rare
For one who strums so dull an air!
     Rubies are Her Highness's lips
     Tra–la–la, and finger tips.
     Diamonds match her sparkling gaze
     Tra–la–la, and witty ways.
     Diamond and ruby-stone
     Are for the Ranee alone!
              Tra–la–la–la–la.

                    M. B.

'Well, I must say I think that's rather nice,' said the
Ranee, 'and shows a very becoming modesty. Muslin and
Vanilla, you can just put the rest of my gift back on my
dressing-table.'

Miss Bianca was rather sorry to hear this, as she'd meant
to turn over all the other jewels as a present to her two
friends. However, Muslin and Vanilla seemed quite delighted by this mark of Her Highness's confidence—and
in fact subsequently wore an extra ring apiece, only Her
Highness didn't notice.

Such was the way of life in the Ranee's palace!

Miss Bianca sighed. One thing she was determined upon was that when she took the 'plane for home again, the emerald should be left behind. She still continued to wear it round her neck, however, at least on duty; and was forced to admit, whenever she passed a mirror, that the quarter-inch square of green fire had probably never looked better than against her own soft, silvery fur.

2

Bernard didn't like it at all.

'I'm sorry to say so, Miss Bianca,' remarked Bernard,

'and I never thought I'd have to say so, but I must say I think you look a bit overdressed.'

'"When in Rome, do as the Romans do",' quoted Miss Bianca lightly. 'And isn't it at least extraordinarily beautiful?'

'I suppose it's beautiful all right,' admitted Bernard.
'Only you don't look like yourself, Miss Bianca, peeping
out over what however beautiful looks to me like a traffic
light . . .'

Miss Bianca didn't feel quite like herself herself. She
wasn't used to taking holidays. In fact the whole atmosphere of the Ranee's palace was already beginning to
remind her of the atmosphere in the salt mine whither
she and Bernard had once penetrated in the interests of
prisoner-rescuing: the same unnatural beauty and tran-
quility, the same ease of living . . .

And the same undercurrent of danger . . .

3

Evidently there were some parts of Ali's tale he hadn't
made up.

Once, as a court poet stumbled over a rhyme—

'I suppose you know,' said the Ranee coldly, 'where
the elephant-lines are?'

'No, Your Highness; that is, yes, Your Highness,'
cringed the poor poet, turning pale.

'And you know what class of persons are sent there?'
continued the Ranee, selecting a crystallized violet.

'Those who have the misfortune—however unwittingly
—to offend Your Highness,' gasped the poet.

'And you know what happens to them at the next full
moon?' continued the Ranee—crunching the violet between her beautiful little sharp teeth. 'If you don't, ask
my Head Pastry Cook! Only of course you can't; good
Hathi trampled him to puff-pastry a fortnight ago. So

you'd better,' concluded the Ranee, 'think quickly of a
more suitable rhyme to "lily" than *"silly"* . . .'

Not unnaturally, the poet was struck dumb. But Miss
Bianca, however horrified, kept her wits.

'*"Chilly"*,' supplied Miss Bianca, in a rapid undertone.
'"Something-something *lily*, then something-something
—never mind about the six syllables!—such as "more fair
and awe-inspiring still. Because so calm and *chilly*."'

'Now that's what I call really clever!' exclaimed the
volatile Ranee, as the poet hastily repeated Miss Bianca's
improvisation. '"Fair and awe-inspiring" is just how I
feel! Fill his mouth with gold!'

The grateful poet attempted to pass at least one of the
gold pieces on to Miss Bianca, but she turned away shud-

dering; and under cover of the general excitement found an opportunity to address Willow at last.

'Can it really be,' murmured Miss Bianca, 'that so dreadful a sentence would indeed have been carried out?'

'Hush!' murmured back Willow. 'Dear little person, try not to think of such things—as I try never to let my girls think of them!'

'No whispering!' snapped the Ranee—her pretty ears evidently as sharp as her pretty teeth. 'Don't you know whispering's *very bad manners?*'

4

'This is a dangerous place indeed,' thought Miss Bianca, 'and thank goodness Bernard has the stables to sneeze in! —I wonder,' she thought suddenly, 'what happened to the cockatoos?'

For a mouse to be haunted by the ghost of a cockatoo was obviously quite ridiculous. Miss Bianca, in bed that night, wasn't precisely haunted—that is, she didn't see cockatoo-shapes or hear cockatoo-voices, but she couldn't help continuing to wonder what had become of them. She knew cockatoos to be exceptionally long-lived birds; the Ambassadress, the Boy's mother, cherished a pink-and-white specimen said to be the same age as the Boy—and he nearly ten. The sleek scarlet feather still dangling from a golden wire suggested birds quite in the prime of life . . .

The answer she got from Vanilla next morning did nothing to make her feel happier.

'Why, they were strangled!' said Vanilla, rather lightly. 'The night someone brought them out for Her Highness's entertainment and the big one fluttered straight into her face!'

'Her Highness fainted three times running and had to be revived with pearls dissolved in wine!' said Muslin.

'When if there's anything Her Highness dislikes it's waste of pearls,' added Vanilla. 'But I do assure you, darling Miss Bianca, the cage was so thoroughly cleaned out afterwards, you're in no slightest danger of catching psittacosis!'

Miss Bianca was glad to hear it. It still pained her to think of the fate of her ex-so-to-speak-landlords; with her usual delicacy, she particularly regretted having christened her inherited residence so light-heartedly. '*Chez* Cockatoo' suggested a cottage *orné*, or small pleasure-house, not the home of martyrs to a Ranee's weak nerves and sense of economy. 'For no doubt 'twas but fright made the poor bird flap in so unfortunate a direction!' thought Miss Bianca. 'How small the offence to bring so great a punishment!'

But that too was the way of life at the Ranee's court. Miss Bianca began to feel very lonely in it. Muslin and Vanilla, however devoted, she couldn't help regarding rather in the light of pets, while with Willow, whom she'd hoped to make a friend, she furthered no more acquaintance, since Willow, (no doubt because her hands were so full), seemed to have been excused attendance in the throne-room altogether.—Plucking the harp-strings in the pianissimo movement of *Le Camembert*, Miss Bianca looked in vain for any other equally sensitive and appreciative face. The Ranee munched pistachio-nuts and crystallized violets: so, encouraged by her example, did all the other ladies; and what annoyed Miss Bianca most of all, not one even noticed if in her natural irritation she struck a false chord . . .

In short, a holiday was a holiday but Miss Bianca couldn't wait to board a west-bound 'plane. She began to count the days; and was thus all the more dismayed when Bernard, when there were only two left to go, suddenly proposed staying on a bit longer.

5

It was a measure of his esteem for Miss Bianca that despite his new obsession with polo Bernard dropped in at *Chez* Cockatoo most mornings. He could never stay long, because the round trip from the stables and back took about seven hours, but unless the Princely Orchids actually had a match, not just a practice, in the afternoon, Bernard made it.

'Well, they beat 'em!' panted Bernard, mopping his brow with his spotted handkerchief (now returned to its natural uses). 'Five goals to one, no less!'

'Who whom?' enquired Miss Bianca politely.

'The Princely Lotuses,' explained Bernard. 'Yesterday, they licked the Princely Tiger-lilies into a cocked hat! After us Orchids they're the hottest bet in the Tournament —and now we'll meet 'em in the Finals next Thursday. My word, what a game that's going to be!'

Miss Bianca paused, mentally counting the days again.

'When I'm sure you'll play a distinguished part,' said she. 'That is, if available. Next Thursday, did you say? By next Thursday, shouldn't we already have boarded the Ambassador's westward-bound 'plane—next Monday?'

'Oh, he's always flipping back and forth,' said Bernard carelessly. 'We'll just catch the next flight out.'

Once more Miss Bianca paused. It may be remembered that she'd hoped a visit to the Orient would broaden Bernard's mind. She hadn't thought of polo as particularly mind-broadening—in fact she hadn't thought of polo at all—but as Bernard went on to remark that he'd sooner be minced to cat-meat than let the team down, and as she recalled that nothing could induce him to play bowls for the M.P.A.S. Bowling Club if he had the Treasurer's accounts to check, she perceived his mind broadened indeed, if in an unexpected direction.

'Anyway you're quite happy here, aren't you, Miss Bianca?' said Bernard. 'You don't *mind* staying a few days longer?'

How could Miss Bianca bear to see his loyal whiskers droop in disappointment? She couldn't.

'Quite!' affirmed Miss Bianca.

Thus it happened that she was still at hand to witness the next, ominous full moon rise over the elephant-lines . . .

8

WORSE STILL!

In the interim Miss Bianca, however distastefully, continued to wear an emerald worth a prince's ransom round her neck, both rubbing her fur and weighing on her spirits; for there is nothing more repugnant to a delicate nature than to have to take a present from someone one dislikes, and by this time Miss Bianca disliked the Ranee almost as much as she'd disliked the jailors in the Black Castle: somehow the Ranee's ravishing beauty made her careless cruelty all the more repellent. Miss Bianca wore the jewel with increasing repugnance; on the other hand, if she hadn't been wearing it, probably the peacock would have simply ignored her . . .

It may also be remembered that to stroke a peacock in its native haunts was something Miss Bianca really wanted to do, and she had been greatly disappointed to find the one woven into the throne-room carpet the single specimen handy. It was upon the terrace outside that the real live peacocks strutted, and hitherto Miss Bianca had been too fully occupied indoors to attempt acquaintance with them. A day or so after her conversation with Bernard, however, she found an opportunity to slip out during the Ranee's afternoon slumbers, and there not a yard distant stood the most magnificent peacock imaginable, just as though waiting by appointment!

'Good day,' said Miss Bianca, with a graceful bow.

After a moment's hesitation, the peacock bowed back.

(It was during this moment that he observed the emerald glittering round her neck and recognized it as a quite extraordinary badge of court favour. On a peacock proud as a peacock it acted as a sort of snobbish charm.)

'My salaams,' said the peacock, bowing back.

His iridescent throat actually brushed the marble pavement.—It was too tempting altogether! Miss Bianca, who had naturally intended to wait until their acquaintance ripened, couldn't resist the opportunity.

'Would you mind if I stroked you?' asked Miss Bianca impulsively. ''Twill fulfil one of my dearest dreams,' she added, 'which I had begun to believe but a dream indeed!'

'Not at all,' said the peacock graciously. (Besides being proud as a peacock he was vain as a peacock.) 'A very natural ambition!'

Delicately Miss Bianca laid her hand on the short blue-green-purple plumage. Delicately stroking, she felt almost an electric shock, such as any contact with sheer beauty always produces in the aesthetically sensitive. Miss Bianca was both aesthetic and sensitive to a high degree—as the peacock at once appreciated. To do him justice, he appreciated it almost as much as he did her jewellery.

'I dare say you'd care to see me unfurl?' he suggested.

'If it's not too much trouble!' begged Miss Bianca.

'Well, I don't usually at this hour,' said the peacock, 'but to please a lady of such obvious taste and discrimination as yourself, here goes!—You'll get a better view if you stand back a bit.'

Upon which, and as Miss Bianca took his advice, slowly and majestically he raised the great multi-coloured fan that was his tail. To Miss Bianca, at ground level, it looked like the Aurora Borealis dyed in rainbows . . .

'Superb!' murmured she. 'Quite, quite superb!'

'I thought you'd enjoy it,' said the peacock. 'With more breeze, I could have shown you something really spectacular. " *The painted sail of a storm-tossed galleon*",' he added musingly, 'to quote another of my admirers who was a poet . . .'

'I myself have ventured into verse,' confessed Miss Bianca.

'One perceived immediately that you were mistress of every elegant and ladylike accomplishment,' returned the peacock courteously.

'Published,' said Miss Bianca.

'Really?' said the peacock, looking at once both surprised and impressed. (He had taken Miss Bianca for a gifted amateur.) 'Actually published?'

'My last slim volume,' recalled Miss Bianca, 'went into three editions; and I believe is actually reprinting.'

'Success indeed!' said the peacock. 'And not only success, fame!—I suppose you couldn't toss off a little impromptu? My wife likes to preserve such things in her Memory Book.'

Miss Bianca rose to the challenge with all an expert's, and artist's pleasure. (Fortunately she'd thought of the Aurora Borealis already.) After but a moment's reflection to get the metre right—

'Why, certainly!' said Miss Bianca,

> *The Northern Lights, th' Aurora Borealis,*
> *Are far less splendid-coloured than your tail is.*

'Charming!' declared the peacock, furling again. 'My wife *will* be pleased!—If you care to stroke my tail-feathers as well, I haven't the least objection.'

Though the big peacock-eyes were now hidden under brown silky fronds, Miss Bianca as she accepted the offer felt the beauty-thrill again. It made her whole journey to the Orient worth while! As they began to stroll on to-gether, chatting of poetry and the charms of Nature, Miss Bianca was really enjoying herself. Miss Bianca quoted a few lines of Keats' 'Ode to a Nightingale', the peacock a whole verse of Hafiz' parallel 'Ode to a Bulbul'. On the cultural plane they grew positively intimate—and even on a lower: turning back from the terrace's limit, the pea-cock quite avuncularly warned Miss Bianca that she shouldn't stray too far outside the palace with such a precious jewel about her neck, in case of thieves.

'Surely *you* shouldn't stray too far either?' said Miss Bianca lightly, 'trailing a whole tailful of gems more precious still!'

She spoke really by way of compliment: to her surprise,

the peacock looked seriously worried.

'It *is* a great responsibility,' he acknowledged. 'You wouldn't believe how constantly on the alert I have to be, not to get it trodden on; for then if I make the least unconsidered movement—my eye-feathers are particularly lightly attached—out comes a whole sheaf to be stolen away and made into fans!'

This was something Miss Bianca hadn't thought of. She was shocked.

'What vandalism!' she exclaimed feelingly. 'I hope such barbarous attempts don't occur often?'

'Well, not so often since Her Highness got rid of that snivelling little page-boy,' said the peacock grimly.

9

WHO IS TELLING LIES?

MISS BIANCA'S whiskers quivered. She paused. (O delightful promenade, so harshly interrupted!)

'A page-boy?' she repeated. 'Why, Her Highness has never had a page-boy!'

'Dear me,' remarked the peacock. 'I wonder who told you that?'

'Why, two of her ladies,' rejoined Miss Bianca. 'By name Muslin and Vanilla.'

'*That* pair of noodles!' said the peacock, with an indulgent smile. 'Very nice, pretty girls I'm sure—but really with no more memory, let alone observation, than a couple of grasshoppers. They haven't a clue as to what goes on in the palace!—No doubt it's in part due to Madam Willow's training,' he added, 'and one can appreciate her motive: our beloved Ranee is so insistent on having only happy faces about her, to learn neither to observe nor remember is probably the first lesson—as the second is to say whatever she, (or indeed anyone else) wants to hear. The poet Omar, now—'

'Pray excuse me,' said Miss Bianca. 'Never has a conversation been more enjoyable; but just at the moment I have rather urgent business indoors.'

With which, after a hurried but still graceful bow, she turned and ran as quickly as she could to find Muslin and Vanilla.

2

Her two friends were in the big marble swimming-pool,
also fortunately alone there. (All the other ladies had suddenly adopted a craze for mah-jongg.) As soon as they saw
Miss Bianca approach, they called to her to come and
join them.

'Come in, Miss Bianca,' called Vanilla, 'and we'll teach
you to float!' (Neither of the pretty creatures had ever

learned to swim.) 'Come in, and we'll dry you afterwards on our own saris!'

'Thank you, not at the moment,' replied Miss Bianca gravely. 'There are times for one sort of thing—such as learning to float—and times for another sort—such as serious conversation.'

Like all frivolous natures, Muslin and Vanilla delighted in the idea of serious conversation. Instantly they were hanging like a couple of mermaids to the marble rim at her feet.—Vanilla still couldn't help kicking a little, to splash a spray of water over Muslin's shoulders, nor could Muslin refrain from splashing Vanilla back. Miss Bianca perceived in short that if she was to get any sense out of them, she must first make the strongest impression possible upon their gentle yet essentially silly minds. She thought rapidly; and like a good general adopted the strategic rather than the tactical approach, which means that instead of at once tackling them on the subject of the page-boy, she sought to impose her authority first.

'Good Muslin, good Vanilla,' said Miss Bianca, 'the time has come to be frank with you: I am not what I seem!'

The result of this impressive statement was rather unexpected. Muslin looked at Vanilla, Vanilla looked at Muslin, then both clapped their hands and burst into peals of delighted laughter.

'We always knew you weren't—didn't we, Muslin?' cried Vanilla. 'We always *knew* you weren't really a mouse, but some enchanted princess under a spell cast by a wicked magician! Only you were so good and beautiful—'

'And sweet and kind—' put in Muslin.

'—he couldn't turn you into a frog—'

'As they usually do!' put in Muslin.

'—only into the prettiest little creature alive! No wonder you need to talk to us seriously! Do, do, darling Miss Bianca—or should we say Your Royal Highness?—tell us just what we must do,' finished Vanilla, 'to help you break the spell!'

With which the pair salaamed as deeply as they could in a swimming-pool, and tried to kiss her hand. Since it was so small, they ended by kissing her all over until she was quite damp.

'Oh, dear!' thought Miss Bianca. 'Both obviously brought up on the Arabian Nights!'—and though their supposition was thus perhaps natural, and certainly flattering, it is always a delicate matter to explain, (without causing disappointment), that instead of being an enchanted princess one is merely the head of a welfare organization. Miss Bianca however saw that she must do so at once, ere misunderstanding thickened like cream into cheese.

'Good Muslin, good Vanilla,' she repeated, 'let me assure you that in one sense I am quite exactly what I am—that is, a mouse from birth.—In fact with a pedigree long as your Ranee's,' smiled Miss Bianca, 'from my ancestress Blanche de Port Salut! I also, however, have the honour to fill the position of Perpetual Madam President of the Mouse Prisoners' Aid Society.'

Fortunately, to Muslin and Vanilla this sounded almost as unusual as being an enchanted princess—indeed *more* unusual; there was nothing about Prisoners' Aid Societies in the Arabian Nights. Miss Bianca, seeing their looks of even deeper interest, felt she could come to the point.

'Thus you may still be of the greatest help,' continued Miss Bianca, 'if not in releasing me from any spell, in assisting me in my present function—beginning by telling me the truth and not simply what you may think I want to hear. Remember our previous conversation on the topic: consider before you reply: there *was*, wasn't there, at least *one* page-boy in the Ranee's service?'

She was prepared to wait several minutes, while the pair considered; but Vanilla answered at once.

'Why, whatever put *that* into your head, darling Miss Bianca-if-not-Your-Royal-Highness-Perpetual-Madam-President?' exclaimed Vanilla, with apparently genuine curiosity.

'I have been talking to a peacock,' said Miss Bianca.

'Then you've been talking to a perfect bird-brain!' declared Vanilla. 'Besides, what can peacocks know about it? In the first place they live outside—don't they, Muslin? A peacock hasn't a clue about what goes on in the palace!'

Just what the peacock had said, reflected Miss Bianca, of Muslin and Vanilla! Who was telling the truth? She in turn began to feel she hadn't a clue, when every single informant, starting with Ali, came to appear so unreliable!

Evidently her drooping whiskers involuntarily betrayed her distressful emotions, for Vanilla and Muslin immediately began kissing her again.

'Don't, please, darling Miss Bianca-if-not-Your-Royal-Highness-Perpetual-Madam-President, look so sad!' begged Vanilla. 'The Ranee might see and be offended!'

'And if she is,' began Muslin fearfully, 'might even—'

'Hush!' interrupted Vanilla. 'And don't *you* start looking sad either! Didn't darling Willow always teach us never to look sad?'

'Also to neither observe nor remember,' suggested Miss Bianca, in her impatience splitting an infinitive. 'My dear

girls, for once in your lives *think*!'
Muslin burst into tears.

'I'm sorry if I spoke harshly—' resumed Miss Bianca.

'It's not *that*!' sobbed Muslin. 'It's—'

'Don't think of it!' said Vanilla quickly.

'But I have!' wailed Muslin. 'I *have* Vanilla, and I know you have too!'

Vanilla began to cry as well. Clinging to each other in the water, they cried and cried . . .

'Really this is excessive,' said Miss Bianca. 'If you have indeed misinformed me, (perhaps owing to some genuine lapse of memory), let us hope 'tis not too late to make amends without breaking your hearts first. I have been making a few calculations: only at full moon, I gather, are sentences actually carried out; therefore since according to Ali the boy's offence occurred some three weeks ago— that is, just after the *last* full moon, not until *this*, the night after next—'

'The night after next!' sobbed Vanilla.

'—is he in absolute peril of his life. There is thus still time to save him,' continued Miss Bianca briskly, 'though no time to be lost; so for goodness' sake stop crying and give me all the relevant information you can.'

But Vanilla and Muslin only sobbed the louder—until at last, and barely gasping the words out—

'You don't *know*, Miss Bianca!' choked Muslin. 'We've tried not to let *ourselves* know! It's darling *Willow* who's in the elephant- lines!'

3

For a moment Miss Bianca was so surprised, shocked

and horrified, she was bereft of speech.—Yet was it not true, she now recalled, that for several days past Willow had been missing from the throne-room? the absence of her sympathetic face indeed quite affecting Miss Bianca's touch on the harp? Yet how to credit such a dreadful circumstance?

'Willow?' repeated Miss Bianca. 'Good, kind, conscientious Willow? How could *she* ever come to deserve such punishment?'

'Don't you remember?' sobbed Vanilla. 'She *whispered* . . .'

'The night the poet rhymed lily wrong,' wept Muslin.

'And Her Highness said it was very bad manners,' sobbed Vanilla.

'So now she's in the elephant-lines,' wept Muslin, 'and the full moon's only two nights off, and though I *know*, Vanilla—it was you who said her name first!—she wouldn't want us to think about her being trampled to smithereens, I *have*—and so have you—and oh, Miss Bianca, there's simply nothing we can do!'

'Perhaps not *you*,' said Miss Bianca, already in full repossession of her faculties, 'but 'tis a type of situation, however poignant, I am reasonably familiar with . . .'

4

All her compassion, indignation and prisoner-rescuing instincts rose to meet the challenge. The page-boy might have existed, or he mightn't: between Ali and the peacock on one hand, and Bernard and Muslin and Vanilla on the other, Miss Bianca still wasn't sure; but Willow un-

doubtedly existed, also Miss Bianca entertained both liking and respect for her.

'Since time is so short, one must begin *at the other end*,' said Miss Bianca decisively. 'That is, by speaking a personal word to Hathi.'

'Only no one ever *can* speak a personal word to him,' mourned Vanilla. 'He's so precious, and valuable, and worth his weight in gold, he's never let stir out without his mahout on his back!'

'I don't suppose his mahout, or driver, spends the whole night there?' said Miss Bianca. 'Once within the elephant-lines by night—'

'Only no one can get *into* the elephant-lines!' despaired Muslin. 'They're too heavily guarded!'

'I know of at least one certain way of gaining entrance,' smiled Miss Bianca. 'By offending the Ranee . . .'

Muslin and Vanilla almost fainted with dismay. Fond as they were of their darling Willow, they were by this time equally fond of their darling Miss Bianca.

'Oh, Miss Bianca, *you* think,' cried Vanilla, 'of what *your* dreadful fate may be!'

'Poohey,' said Miss Bianca. (She didn't usually employ such vulgar expressions, also was well aware of the danger she courted, but wished to startle Muslin and Vanilla, for their own sakes, from looking so unhappy.) 'Poohey!' repeated Miss Bianca. 'I shall offend Her Highness this very evening!'

10

INTO THE JAWS OF ELEPHANTS!

She was as good as her word. She had played Greensleeves once, *Le Camembert* twice: as the Ranee demanded
a third rendering of that delightful air—

'I'm so sorry,' said Miss Bianca, 'I'm too tired.'

She rose from the harp. For a moment there was such
silence, the last twang of a golden string seemed to re-echo
on the air. Muslin and Vanilla put their arms round each
other.

'Too tired to play for *Her Highness*?' gasped one of the
ladies at last.

'Of course I'm dreadfully sorry,' said Miss Bianca
lightly—so lightly that she didn't really sound sorry at all.

The Ranee's beautiful swallow-wing eyebrows drew
together in a frown. Vanilla and Muslin clung closer still,
while all the rest of the ladies tried to hide behind each
other's backs.

'Be careful you don't offend me,' said the Ranee. 'You
know what happens to people who offend me?'

'As I understand,' said Miss Bianca, 'they're sent to the
elephant-lines to be trampled to smithereens. But really
in my present state of fatigue *anything* is preferable to
playing *Le Camembert* again. In fact, I won't.'

A sigh like wind over reeds shook the whole court. But
none, to Miss Bianca's surprise, sighed louder than the
Ranee!

'I think you're being very inconsiderate,' complained
the Ranee, 'to force my hand so. Of course I always knew

you'd have to be retired eventually, but I meant to have you stuffed. Trampled by Hathi, there wouldn't be a morsel left of your nice coat!'

'Look rather on the bright side,' encouraged Miss Bianca. 'I don't believe I should stuff at all well—and you wouldn't wish me preserved looking less than my best?'

'Oh, as to that,' said the Ranee, 'my taxidermist is quite *brilliant*. You should see how beautifully he did the cockatoos! Really they look far more handsome than in life.'

'But consider the difference in size,' pointed out Miss Bianca. 'Cockatoos are practically poultry-sized; any competent cook could stuff a cockatoo.' (Though she regretted speaking so disrespectfully of her ex-landlords, she felt that in the circumstances they would understand and forgive.) 'To stuff a mouse,' continued Miss Bianca, 'is so much more fiddling; as I'm sure any taxidermist would find.'

Unfortunately this plausible argument met an equally plausible rejoinder.

'*My* taxidermist,' observed the Ranee, 'can stuff humming-birds—only look at that sweet little row of them holding up my gauze! I'm sure he'd make something really artistic of you; perhaps seated at the harp. In fact,' concluded the Ranee, 'and even though it means breaking with precedent, you *shan't* be sent to the elephant-lines; you shall be drowned—without damage to a single hair! And just to show how merciful I am,' she added, 'in rose-water in a silver bowl, and by your two particular friends Muslin and Vanilla.'

What could Miss Bianca do but bow her appreciation? (Vanilla and Muslin, despite Willow's teaching, barely restrained their tears.)

'Not only merciful, but thoughtful,' said Miss Bianca. 'After such kind consideration I only hope I may stuff quite exquisitely!' She paused. 'All the same,' she reflected, 'shouldn't we wait but another day, for the full moon?—since I understand that only at her plentitude are such sentences usually executed?'

'No, we shouldn't,' said the Ranee. '*This* next full moon doesn't rise till midnight[1], so it's far *more* than a day, and in any case I'm never to be kept waiting a minute. Someone fetch a bowl of rose-water!'

Miss Bianca shrugged.

'Just as you like,' said she. 'But though Your Highness, out of the goodness of Your Highness's heart, may be prepared to break with *one* precedent, is it not ever rash, in Royalty, to depart from protocol altogether?'

By protocol Miss Bianca meant the usual way of doing things at Courts, any departure from which might attract the notice of the populace and start it wondering whether Courts were really worth while.—The Ranee, who in her own selfish way was quite clever, paused in turn; then bade Muslin and Vanilla, instead of drowning Miss Bianca at once, to keep her in strict custody a day and a half longer; also promised to give a little party amongst intimates to witness the pretty ceremony planned.

2

'Dear me, how tiresome!' said Miss Bianca.

Vanilla, in the act of popping her tenderly into strict custody in *Chez* Cockatoo, gazed in tearful admiration.

---

[1] Actually a full moon normally rises about sunset, but this happened to be that rarity a blue one. Hence the expression 'Once in a blue moon.'

'I don't know how you can be so brave, Miss Bianca,' marvelled Vanilla. 'I suppose it comes with practice; for I'm sure Muslin and I couldn't call it just *tiresome*, if *we* were going to be drowned in rose-water. Even having to drown *you* in rose-water is too, too dreadful—isn't it, Muslin?'

'My dear girls,' said Miss Bianca, 'by "tiresome" I referred not to the prospect of my immediate if fragrant death, (which I can assure is most unlikely to occur), but to the temporary hitch in my designs. However, if the Ranee won't send me to the elephant-lines, I must think of some other means of entering them, and in fact have done so already. You shall take me there yourselves.'

Muslin looked at Vanilla. Vanilla looked at Muslin. It was as if the same shudder shook them both.

'But we can't, Miss Bianca! We don't know the way!' protested Muslin.

'Of course you do,' said Miss Bianca briskly. 'After so long in the palace, of course you must know at least the *way* to the elephant-lines, even if you haven't actually visited them.'

'It's through the big arch beyond the stables,' admitted Vanilla.

'Which since Bernard has no difficulty in getting here *from*, there can be no difficulty in getting from here *to*,' said Miss Bianca. ''Tis true it takes him half a day, but to you 'twould be no more than half an hour; and as there's no time to lose I must ask you to carry me there at once. Only be brave—'

'Only we *aren't*!' cried Vanilla desperately. 'We just *aren't* brave—are we, Muslin?'

There was no need for Muslin's affirmative nod. If

Vanilla was shuddering again, Muslin's teeth were now positively chattering. Never had Miss Bianca encountered such a brace of poltroons! Then suddenly the recollection stirred of how little courageous she'd been herself, the first time she'd embarked on a heroic enterprise. When Bernard—how long ago!—first came to ask her help in rescuing a Norwegian poet from the Black Castle, hadn't the now famous intrepid Miss Bianca actually fainted from terror? And how had she been persuaded to undertake that enterprise? By an appeal not to her courage, but to her compassion . . .

'My dears,' said Miss Bianca, in her sweetest and most silvery tones, 'as Vanilla just said, being brave, (like playing the harp), comes only by practice. Why shouldn't you both begin to practise now—especially in the interest of your darling Willow?'

This appeal too was not without effect. Even a chicken-heart may be also a truly fond one.

'Darling Willow!' murmured Vanilla.

'Darling Willow!' echoed Muslin.

'Who held your hands,' reminded Miss Bianca, 'when you were so young you cried in bed . . .'

Vanilla looked at Muslin; Muslin looked at Vanilla; while Miss Bianca waited anxiously—because if *they* wouldn't carry her to the elephant-lines, however was she to get there in time? Then suddenly, in the same sniff—

'We'll try!' sniffed Muslin and Vanilla.

4

Undoubtedly it was a splendid start at being brave, to

carry Miss Bianca out into and across the palace gardens. Fortunately it wasn't dark—both Muslin and Vanilla were afraid of the dark—the moon being but a night from full; yet in a way this made things worse, since the party could be more easily observed by a patrolling watchman. But with their hearts in their mouths, (and Miss Bianca in a fold of Vanilla's sari), they slipped from the shadow of one rose-bush to the next, then into the shadow of a lilac-alley, and so gained the stables.

In a little snuggery under the harness-room floor Bernard was swapping jokes with his fellow polo-players. Little did he guess that Miss Bianca was so nigh, or what she was up to!

The stable watchman *did* observe them. Luckily he took Muslin and Vanilla, in their pale draperies, for two ghosts. He disappeared as swiftly as a ghost himself ere beyond, at last, loomed the huge granite archway.

It was heavily barred, but of course Miss Bianca could get through.

'Here set me down,' said she. 'And my dears, you've not only been brave, you've been positive heroines! Why, you needed no practice at all!—many a hero of antiquity could take a lesson from you!'

At this well-deserved praise, both beamed with such pride, pleasure, self-satisfaction (and why not?) and enthusiastic co-operativeness, no one would have taken them for the same girls who half an hour earlier could only shiver and shake! But such is often the result of trying.

'We'll wait for you till you get back,' said Vanilla. 'Won't we, Muslin?'

Miss Bianca gave each a kiss and slipped through the bars. She had often been in the jaws of death before, (counting bloodhounds), but never yet in the jaws, or rather upon the tusks, of elephants. She advanced none the less with all her usual coolness in the jaws of anything.

HATHI

IMMEDIATELY, however, Miss Bianca wondered whether her friends hadn't by mistake introduced her not into the elephant-lines at all, but rather into the aisle of some great cathedral lined with double granite pillars on each side. As first one pillar, then the next, began to twitch and shift, Miss Bianca very much hoped there wasn't going to be an earthquake. Then she perceived that the base of each column had toe-nails on it—each to Miss Bianca big as a barn door, but undoubtedly toe-nails—and realized not only that what she'd taken for the supports of a sacred edifice were in fact the back legs of twenty or so elephants, but also that it was probably her own miniscule presence that made them tremble so. 'I must certainly tell Bernard,' thought Miss Bianca, 'who has never really believed elephants to be afraid of mice, that I produced quite the effect of an earthquake!'

This wasn't strictly true, since it was she herself who had thought of earthquakes, not the elephants. But what was true was that all the elephants were nervous because they felt there was a mouse about, while Miss Bianca was so heartened, she ran on with ever-increasing confidence.

There was no sign of Willow.—This Miss Bianca had expected: obviously prisoners waiting to be trampled to smithereens wouldn't be held actually *in* the elephant-lines—there wouldn't be accommodation, also the elephants might get fond of them—but in some adjacent

prison; what she hadn't expected, however, was the total absence of guards. In fact the stable guard had loyally rushed to inform his colleagues that there were ghosts abroad, and all the elephant-line guards had vamoosed along with him to a safe distance. But though she didn't guess the reason, Miss Bianca was heartened afresh; and finally approached the very biggest elephant, Hathi, the Ranee's favourite, without having turned a whisker.

He was so big she couldn't see all of him at once. Miss Bianca still felt slightly like a tourist in a cathedral as she tiptoed between his back legs, then his front, admiring, so to speak, the architecture. When she ran up on his manger it was like confronting a stained-glass window!—for Hathi's trunk and forehead and ears alike were painted all over with patterns of scarlet and green. The aim of this decoration, when the Ranee rode out on his back, was to produce in the beholder not only admiration but awe: Miss Bianca however was too sophisticated to feel either of these emotions. She in fact thought Hathi would look better left in his native state of granite-greyness. Certainly she wasn't awed at all, but rather held herself ready to comfort and reassure should her sudden appearance at close quarters have the effect she now confidently anticipated.—It had. No sooner did he set eyes on her than the enormous pachyderm began quaking all over from the tip of his trunk to the root of his tail. His thick skin rippled like lava, his flanks heaved in and out. It was like seeing Vesuvius about to erupt, or an iceberg about to calve, or any other tremendous force of nature in violent convulsion.

'Go away! Don't come near me! Fetch my mahout!' squealed Hathi.—Miss Bianca was surprised to hear his voice so shrill; she'd expected it to be as deep as Chaliapine's. (Miss Bianca often went to the Opera, at a matinée, in the Boy's pocket, and the great Russian *basso profundo* had made a strong impression on her. Otherwise she'd probably have expected a voice just as deep as a fog-horn.)

'Pray be under no apprehension!' said Miss Bianca. 'I won't hurt you! All I seek is a little chat, and perhaps co-operation.—Though why any person of *your* size,' she added curiously, 'should be apprehensive of anyone mouse-size, I confess I find difficult to understand?'

'*You* weren't in the Ark,' snuffled Hathi, calming down a bit, but still nervously.

'Nor you either, I suppose!' smiled Miss Bianca. 'And surely whatever happened in the Ark is too long ago to bother about now?'

'An elephant never forgets,' returned Hathi. 'How a couple of mice, in the Ark, drove my I-don't-know-how-many-great-great-great-grandparents nearly overboard by playing hide-and-seek in their ears is something I for one shan't ever forget if I live to be old as Methusalah.— And it wasn't only us elephants who complained to Noah,' he went on, now seeming quite pleased to have someone to talk, or rather grumble, to. 'The zebras complained as well, about hop scotch on their stripes. There was quite a petition got up to Noah, to send those two *mice* swimming out to sea and see what *they*'d bring back, instead of nice inoffensive Mrs Dove!'

Though it was a bad beginning, Miss Bianca collected her wits and employed all her well-known tact.

'I see you have good reason for your suspicions,' she said soothingly, 'and must really apologize on behalf of my whole race! But since those days I'm sure you'll find us grown better-mannered: in my *own* memory I can't recall a single instance of a mouse driving an elephant to near self-destruction in the way you so feelingly describe.'

'I dare say *your* memory isn't very long,' said Hathi unconvincedly. 'I dare say there's been hundreds. In fact it's a thing I'd rather not discuss, because I happen to be very sensitive and tender-hearted to a fault.'

At this Miss Bianca absolutely lost patience with him.

'An elephant, and you call yourself sensitive!' she exclaimed indignantly. 'An elephant, and you call yourself tender-hearted—you who trample people to smithereens!'

To her astonishment, at these stinging words Hathi looked neither ashamed, nor angry, nor contrite, but simply and utterly astounded.

2

'Trample *people*?' he repeated incredulously. 'Us elephants trample *people*? Goodness me, we'd never think of such a thing! A tiger, perhaps, in self-defence—'

'But you do, you know,' said Miss Bianca. 'I'm afraid it's only too well authenticated. You yourself are on record as having—' she shuddered delicately—'made puff-pastry of Her Highness's Head Pastry Cook.'

'Whenever?' demanded Hathi indignantly.

'At last full moon,' said Miss Bianca.

He thought for a moment; then looked relieved.

'Oh, *that*!' said Hathi. 'Why, that was just a tidying-up job on the new airstrip. Some ill-conditioned person had left a great bundle of rubbish and so on bang in the middle, and I was asked if I'd mind just going along after hours to stamp it nice and flat. Of course a full moon always rather dazzles me; I just shut my eyes and stamped; but I do honestly assure you it was just a tidying-up job.'

Alas, thought Miss Bianca, how even the best-hearted —for she felt sure Hathi was good at heart—could be misled into performing the cruellest actions, if only they were told they were doing something else and didn't look for themselves! ''Tis how half the evil in the world is done,' thought Miss Bianca sadly, 'by the innocent to the innocent . . .' It struck her indeed that the Head Pastry Cook mightn't have been entirely innocent—might have sold cakes on the side, or skimped and stolen the butter—such was the way of life at the Ranee's court!—but the thought brought no consolation; if he'd been a Christian martyr Hathi would have trampled him just the same, under the impression of doing something praiseworthy . . .

'I do hope you believe me?' pressed Hathi, evidently a little worried by her silence.

'Yes, indeed,' said Miss Bianca. 'I do indeed believe you, poor Hathi! In fact, at next full moon, (actually to-morrow), in case there's any *more* rubbish to be tidied, it would give me pleasure to accompany you and watch in person. In the capital where I usually reside, rubbish-disposal is such a problem, I should be glad to pick up a few hints to transmit to the Municipal Authorities . . .'

She chose her words wisely. Big words like Municipal Authorities always impress an elephant.

'I should be honoured,' said Hathi.—A last uncontroll-able shudder none the less rippled his hide. 'When you say *accompany* me,' he added nervously, 'you don't mean *on* me?'

'Certainly I do,' said Miss Bianca. (At ground level on the air strip, Hathi trampling conscientiously about, she'd probably have been the first casualty.) 'As I remarked earlier, whatever occurred in the Ark is surely too long ago to affect our present relationship! Forget the Ark!— Hold out your trunk, let me run just once up and down it, and I'm sure you'll never be frightened of a mouse again!'

It quite amused Miss Bianca to think that after teaching Muslin and Vanilla to be brave, she was now teaching an elephant to be! But though this may sound absurd, it was actually the most courageous thing Hathi had ever achieved in his life, as after a moment's hesitation he did as Miss Bianca invited. He had often been courageous before, while he was still wild, fighting off tigers—but that was in hot blood, and in any case something expected of elephants. All his relations would have been ashamed of him if he hadn't fought courageously. Now he had to overcome not only an inherited fear of mice, but also the fear of what those same relations would say if they heard of his actually fraternizing with one. It called for a different kind of courage, the sort known as moral, and which is often harder to produce than the bang-and-bang-back sort. But under the influence of Miss Bianca's personality and eloquence, Hathi suddenly felt brave all round.

Miss Bianca was pretty brave too. Hathi's extended trunk swayed before her like a suspension-bridge; the red and green zigzags with which it was painted affected her as a motorist might have been affected by traffic lights stuck simultaneously at Stop and Go. Summoning all her poise and courage, however, she positively tripped, light as a feather, across the rubbery surface; paused a moment, to take breath, on the belvedere of Hathi's forehead, and

as lightly tripped back without even making him sneeze.

'So you see,' smiled Miss Bianca, 'it wasn't so dreadful after all!'

'Actually it felt rather nice,' confessed Hathi. 'Like when Mummy used to stroke a headache away . . . You can come and ride on me whenever you like!'

'I shall take you at your word!' called Miss Bianca, as she scampered back towards the archway.

3

On its further side Muslin and Vanilla were waiting just as promised. They hadn't even been *bored*, they assured Miss Bianca; in fact, (their frivolous natures re-asserting themselves), they'd had a thoroughly enjoyable time pretending to be ghosts and going *Boo-hoo* to scare off any returning conscientious guard who showed his nose . . .

'If you'd only seen them,' giggled Vanilla, scooping

Miss Bianca up again, 'when Muslin went *Boo-hoo-Boo*!'

Actually Miss Bianca hadn't time to recount her own experiences, as ere the party recrossed the stables they overtook Bernard making for *Chez* Cockatoo. It could have been quite a gay reunion, only Bernard obviously felt otherwise.

'If you wanted a look at the stables, Miss Bianca,' said he, in a huffish tone, 'I'd have been only too happy to show you round myself. I've *wanted* to show you round, only I thought the trip might be too tiring.'

'So it would indeed,' agreed Miss Bianca. 'Which is why I have availed myself of Muslin and Vanilla's kindness . . .'

'I still think you might have told me you were coming,' said Bernard.

He sounded not only huffish but hurt. Miss Bianca ran lightly down Vanilla's sari, to be able to talk to him face to face instead of *de haut en bas*.

'I thought you'd be playing polo,' she explained—not quite truthfully, because in fact ever since hearing of Willow's plight she'd been too preoccupied to give a thought to Bernard at all. 'Isn't it the Final?'

'The Final,' said Bernard, 'is tomorrow. In the afternoon. That's why I started so early to come and see you, so as to get back in time to get a bit of a rest first.'

Miss Bianca was really touched. She knew how much the Finals meant to him—yet to visit her in *Chez* Cockatoo he had been prepared to spend almost the whole morning hiking!

'Dear Bernard,' said she, 'do pray forgive my foolish, female confusion! And since we happen to have met here and now, why not take advantage of the circumstance, and without foregoing our usual pleasant chat spare you further exertion? I'm sure our friends won't mind waiting a little longer!'

So speaking, she sank gracefully down on a nicely-rounded cobblestone, and of course Bernard did the same, while Muslin and Vanilla amused themselves by draping the hems of their saris in a little surrounding tent. It was really just as cosy and private as at *Chez* Cockatoo.

'I'm sorry if I sounded cross,' said Bernard.

''Twas only natural,' said Miss Bianca. 'And how good of you to contemplate the journey at all, in such circumstances!'

'Well, to be honest,' said honest Bernard honestly, 'I nearly didn't contemplate it, before the Final; only I specially wanted to tell you, something I overheard from that chauffeur, that the Ambassador's 'plane didn't leave last Tuesday after all. It leaves tomorrow midnight instead, and I thought you'd want us to take it.'

'Twas the very news Miss Bianca needed, to enable her to extend her audacious plan for saving Willow's life into one for rescuing her altogether!

4

'Certainly we should take it!' exclaimed Miss Bianca. 'Actually at midnight, you say?'

'Well, plus half an hour,' said Bernard. 'And I know what you're thinking, Miss Bianca, because I've thought of it myself: what a glorious sight it's going to be as up we soar in the light of the full moon!'

Of course Miss Bianca did thoroughly look forward to such a sight—but what she was actually thinking was that such a schedule allowed time to embark Willow on board the 'plane too!

'So I'll come and fetch you straight away after the match,' went on Bernard, 'even if it means missing—whether we win or lose, though in my opinion it's a cert —a bit of a celebration. Just have your bag ready packed.'

'Don't think of it,' said Miss Bianca hastily. 'Vanilla and Muslin will I'm sure again offer their services, so why not let us simply meet at the airstrip? In fact, I'll join you on the 'plane.'

Bernard found this a very good idea. Besides sparing Miss Bianca fatigue, it meant he needn't miss the celebration, also several members of the polo team had promised to come and see him off, and he felt he wouldn't at all mind them seeing him, besides off, seen off by two such beauties as Muslin and Vanilla as well.

Little did he guess that Miss Bianca planned to gain the aircraft not at the pretty hands of ladies, but on elephant-back!

12

THE WAITING HOURS

MISS BIANCA in fact never returned to *Chez* Cockatoo at all. As soon as Bernard had bidden her a fond (temporary) farewell—

'My dears,' Miss Bianca told Muslin and Vanilla, 'I have decided 'twill be wiser for me, during the next elapsing hours, to shun the palace altogether. My conversation with Hathi has been fruitful indeed; there is every hope of Willow's safety; but I cannot risk Her Highness's suddenly jumping the gun and ordering me drowned in rose-water ahead of time. I therefore propose to return with you no further than the garden-limit, where in some rustic nook to wait out the day. In short, my dears, this is where we part.'

For a wonder—or perhaps it wasn't such a wonder, now that they'd learnt to be brave—neither Muslin nor Vanilla burst into tears.

'We always knew you'd vanish some time—didn't we, Muslin?' sighed Vanilla.

'As enchanted princesses always do!' sighed Muslin. (She at least, however newly-brave, still under the influence of the Arabian Nights.) 'But isn't there anything we can fetch you, Miss Bianca, like light lunch or your overnight bag?'

Miss Bianca hesitated. For luncheon she had no doubt of finding a sprig of wild parsley—notoriously full of vitamins—to nibble, whereas her overnight bag she was really attached to. But a point much on her mind was the consequences to her friends when the Ranee found the centrepiece, so to speak, of a little intimate drowning-party lacking . . . After a moment's thought, Miss Bianca slipped the emerald ring from about her neck and deposited it beside Vanilla's toes.

'The Ranee's jewel,' said Miss Bianca, 'I leave as a gift between you. I know you won't quarrel over it! But will it suffice, should the Ranee turn her anger upon you, to bribe your way to freedom out of the elephant-lines?'

Vanilla looked at Muslin. Muslin looked at Vanilla.

'Actually,' confessed Vanilla, 'we've often thought—haven't we, Muslin?—of all sorts of things we could do with it. Muslin has an uncle who's a jeweller—'

'And Vanilla has an uncle who's a farmer—' put in Muslin.

'And if we sold it to Muslin's uncle, and took a whole bag of gold back to *my* uncle, we could marry the two handsomest boys in my uncle's village! We've even thought of how we could get away—by putting on quite shabby saris and mixing with the cowherds who come at dawn to bring milk. But until you've now taught us to be brave, Miss Bianca, we'd never have done it!'

'And anyway we hadn't *got* the emerald,' pointed out Muslin, with unexpected practicality. 'You do really and truly, Miss Bianca, give it us?'

'With all my heart!' declared Miss Bianca.—'See, dawn begins to break already,' she added, 'and I'm sure your saris, after such a night's adventuring, look quite shabby enough as it is! Take the jewel and run as fast as you can, my dears, join the cowherds without delay, and don't give another thought to my overnight bag!'

Muslin and Vanilla at once obeyed her instructions.—
Vanilla stooped for the emerald ring and tied it in a corner
of her sari, letting Muslin hold the knot, then they kissed
Miss Bianca most fervently, and ran as fast as they could
to mingle with the cowherds, and so no more than Miss
Bianca ever returned to the Ranee's cruel palace.

2

At the garden limit weeds rioted. Miss Bianca had no
difficulty in finding herself a hammock among convol-
vuluses wherein to doze out the rest of the day ere midnight, with all its attendant perils, loomed—and what
better interim resource than poetry?

POEM BY MISS BIANCA COMPOSED WHILE
WAITING TO BOARD AN AEROPLANE
BY ELEPHANT

Rocking to and fro, to and fro, to and fro,
> (murmured Miss Bianca to herself)
Rocking to and fro, where the big blue blossoms blow—

'*I*'d say, "on the go",' remarked a passing bee. '*I*'m always on the go!'

'Indeed quite a proverb for it,' said Miss Bianca, rather shortly. 'Don't let me detain you!'

Swinging high and low, high and low, high and low
> (she continued)
Swinging high and low, where the tall grasses grow
In the shade unafraid of the sun!

She hadn't realized there was a lizard so close.

'You've got it the wrong way round,' criticized the lizard. 'It ought to be 'in the *sun* unafraid of the *shade*!'

Miss Bianca was unused to composing poetry so to speak in public, and after this second interruption went on inside her head.

No sweeter spot to wait in,
Relax and meditate in,
Till the long hours of waiting have run!

> M. B.

She composed several other verses, all in the same lulling rhythm, and in fact halfway through the fifth had lulled herself to sleep. Which was just as well, considering her exertions of the previous night, also what exertions lay before her!

Miss Bianca in fact slept until past sundown, and long after that; absolutely until the skies lightened with adumbrant moonrise . . .

'Good gracious!' thought Miss Bianca, hurrying back across the stables, 'what if I had overslept! How many a slip there is indeed, betwixt cup and lip!'

She spoke more prophetically than she knew!

13

THE CUP AND THE LIP

BEYOND the archway into the elephant-lines there seemed
to be a good deal of activity. Hathi was out of his stall, his
driver already mounted, while in the other stalls other
mahouts moved nervously about trying to keep their
elephants quiet. As all down the lines trunks quivered and
tails switched, 'twas less like being in a cathedral, thought
Miss Bianca, than in a forest with a storm blowing up . . .

'And I don't believe 'tis on my account either!' thought she—but not with any offended vanity; she was only too glad to be able to run up and take station behind Hathi's left ear unobserved. Even his mahout, an elderly, grim-faced man, didn't observe her; in fact he had an oddly drowsy look that for a moment suggested to Miss Bianca that perhaps he'd been refreshing himself with something stronger than either coffee or sherbet; then she charitably put it down to the lateness of the hour.

'Here I am!' whispered Miss Bianca, into the great big-as-a-banana-leaf ear-flap. (Painted now, she observed, not with red and green but black and purple. So were his trunk and forehead painted in the same funereal colours.)

'I began to think you'd forgotten,' mumbled Hathi. 'And I still can't think why you want to come along on just a little tidying-up job . . .'

'Call it feminine caprice,' said Miss Bianca. 'You who so often carry the Ranee must surely know what *that* means!'

'Mostly being kow-towed to in bazaars,' mumbled Hathi. 'However, if *your* caprice is to watch me doing sweeper's work, hold tight!'

With that he swung into the long, rocking elephant-stride that affects some passengers like the motion of a ship at sea. But Miss Bianca had been to sea, and knew just how to keep balance. As Hathi lunged first to port, then to star-board, she preserved all her customary aplomb, both mental and physical.

Only how brilliant and startling rose the Oriental full moon! More startling still because slightly blue! Even through her thick dark lashes Miss Bianca was almost dazzled, while she felt quite sure Hathi was!

There were other illuminations. As they approached the new airstrip, on the old one adjoining Miss Bianca could see the lights of the 'plane that presumably had the Oriental Ambassador, also Bernard, already on board. Besides seeing, she could hear; and across the short distance, what she feared she heard was the sound of its propellers experimentally revving up . . .

Hathi paused to ask if she were quite comfortable.

'Perfectly!' said Miss Bianca. 'Pray don't go slowly on my account! In fact, couldn't you hurry a little?'

But nothing can make an elephant hurry when he doesn't want to, and evidently Hathi wasn't wanting to. On he rocked a few strides more, then paused again.

'I don't know why,' mumbled Hathi, 'but somehow I just don't feel like trampling tonight. Anyway, *I* can't see any rubbish lying about.'

Naturally, thought Miss Bianca, moon-dazzled as he was! Or could it be a subconscious bad conscience suddenly operating? ('If so, how untimely!' thought Miss Bianca.) But *she* could see, and what she saw made her throw into her next words all the persuasiveness and urgency possible.

'Good Hathi, do pray proceed!' begged Miss Bianca. 'For in the airstrip's very centre *I* perceive some obstruction indeed!'

'Oh, all right!' grumbled Hathi, 'but I may as well do it with my eyes shut and just let old Surly guide me!'

On he lumbered again towards the centre of the airstrip; where lay besides the bound-hand-and-foot figure of Willow a *bound-hand-and-foot little boy in tatters of white and cherry-coloured silk*!

As his mahout halted him—

'This the place?' muttered Hathi.

'Yes!' screamed Miss Bianca, running down his trunk and beginning to nibble feverishly at the bonds. 'Yes, yes, yes, Hathi! The place, and the *people*—whom, instead of trampling, you shall bear to safety! Open your eyes and gather us up!'

'Shan't,' said Hathi, with a sudden return of obstinacy. 'In fact, I shan't do anything more at all. I shall just stop as I am, and go to sleep until I feel the sun nice and hot on my back in the morning . . .'

Not Miss Bianca's renewed pleas could stir him, nor the mahout's cruel goad, as there stood Hathi indifferent and immovable while the propellers revved up for the last time.

2

The aircraft was all set to go. The Captain, with the few minutes in hand he always allowed himself, was taking a last stroll and a last few gulps of fresh air. So was the Air Hostess, a little way behind.

Bernard, who couldn't imagine what had happened to Miss Bianca, was so desperate he tried to run back down the gangway, only his enthusiastic supporters from the Mouse Oriental Polo Club got in the way. He was actually at fisticuffs with them, but very heavily outnumbered.

The Captain turned back. In exactly three minutes he would be in his seat at the controls and Miss Fitzpatrick heating tinned soup and the aircraft airborne—and Miss Bianca and Willow and the page-boy left irretrievably behind!

3

Suddenly the Captain halted.

'Good heavens!' he exclaimed. 'What is this I see?'

Well might he exclaim! There in front of the propellers the mustard-and-cress sown by Miss Bianca had sprouted in three universally-recognized letters . . .

'I say, Miss Fitzpatrick!' called the Captain, 'just come and take a look at this! Do you see what I see?'

'Certainly,' said the hostess. 'It's mustard-and-cress.

I've sown it myself, for my baby brother's initials.'

'Perhaps one of the locals,' suggested the Captain, 'has a baby brother named Selim Ozmandias Sennacherib?'

But he spoke more lightly than he felt, and Miss Fitzpatrick knew it. The letters *might* represent the initials of a Selim Ozmandias Sennacherib: what they did beyond doubt represent was the universally-recognized signal meaning HELP!—exactly as Miss Bianca had intended they should when she sowed them on the very moment of arrival, just in case.

'S.O.S.' said the Captain uneasily.

'S.O.S. it is,' agreed Miss Fitzpatrick.

'Everyone aboard all right?' asked the Captain. 'No one left behind?'

'If they were, they'd hardly have time to grow mustard-and-cress,' said Miss Fitzpatrick practically. 'Anyway I've seen the Ambassador into his berth and ticked off every member of his suite. All the same—'

'All the same?' prompted the Captain.

'All the same,' suggested the Hostess, 'mightn't we wait

just a few minutes longer, and catch up over the Indian Ocean?'

4

Thus it was that the 'plane still hadn't taken off when Miss Bianca employed her last desperate resource and by a sharp nip on the tender tip of Hathi's trunk managed to rouse him from his selfish somnolence.—It was purely from pain that he opened his eyes; but when he did, and saw not rubbish but human forms lying in his path, his remorse and anger knew no bounds.

'This is awful!' Hathi trumpeted his distress abroad. 'I've been deceived!'—With a furious shrug he chucked the mahout clean off his back. 'Us elephants don't trample *people*! Or if I ever have by mistake, only tell me what I can do now to make amends!'

Miss Bianca told him at once. Down and aloft wreathed Hathi's trunk, scooping up Willow and the page-boy and Miss Bianca ere he braced himself for the charge. . . .

5

'If you see what I see,' said the Air Hostess, with her customary calm, 'there seems to be an elephant charging us. He's not on the list; should I try to berth him amidships?'

'Good heavens, we'd never get off the ground!' cried the Captain. 'Fetch His Excellency at once and tell him absolutely no zoological specimens allowed!—No, there isn't time,' decided the Captain. 'Just stand clear of the doors, Miss Fitzpatrick, and gangway up!'

14

THE END

BUT what was a chuck of a few yards to an elephant?
With an easy twirl of his powerful trunk Hathi gently
lofted in his three passengers just ere the cabin door closed,
then rumbled a courteous farewell to Miss Bianca, and
swayed back under the moonlight to his own quarters.
Contrary to Miss Fitzpatrick's and the Captain's appre-
hensions, he'd never intended boarding the 'plane himself·
it looked to him too much like a Noah's Ark.

2

Now it was that the Air Hostess's wonderful qualities
showed at their best—that is, she completely disregarded
all regulations about not taking passengers on board without tickets. Confronted by two obviously-suffering
fellow-creatures—Willow and the page-boy—Miss Fitzpatrick simply put them in the two nearest empty seats
and adjusted their safety-belts. (There were plenty of
empty seats, since only the Ambassador and his suite were
officially travelling.) Then she splashed Willow with
lavender-water, popped a barley-sugar sweet into the
page-boy's mouth, and opened two more tins of soup. The
one thing Miss Fitzpatrick didn't do was make her way
forward and report to the Captain, since any ignoring of
the regulations on *his* part might well cost him his Cap-

taincy, and she had his interests truly at heart.

'Sleep as long as you can, poor lady!' murmured Miss Fitzpatrick to Willow, as she finally flicked the cabin lights off. 'And you too, you poor little urchin! I'll not trouble you with cleaning up till morning!—Now don't tell me it's the pair of *you* here again!' she added, with a change of tone, as entering her own private cubicle there she saw Bernard and Miss Bianca sitting side by side on her box of Kleenex . . .

3

Their reunion had been rather tempestuous. Naturally the nerves of both were a little on edge, and their tempers a little frayed: to Miss Bianca's cold enquiry as to why Bernard had so nearly let the aircraft leave without her, Bernard had hotly replied that people who preferred to catch an aeroplane by elephant should at least employ punctual elephants; also that the very moment he realized her overdue, he'd tried to scrum down to look for her through practically the whole Mouse Oriental Polo Club.

'In fact brawling,' said Miss Bianca coldly. 'Good Hathi I admit may have been a little dilatory—'

'The big brute!' snarled Bernard.

'—but how effectual his aid at last!' pointed out Miss Bianca. 'Never mind, my dear Bernard; here I am, thanks to Hathi, safe and sound!'

'But I do mind!' cried Bernard. 'It should have been thanks to me!—O Miss Bianca, if you only knew what agonies I went through, (besides most of the Mouse Oriental Polo Club), when for several dreadful moments

I thought perhaps we'd never see each other again! I began to tear my whiskers out by the roots!—Just look, Miss Bianca!' cried Bernard. 'It was my very longest!'

There indeed it lay between them on the Kleenex—Bernard's longest whisker. How could Miss Bianca, who knew what pride he'd taken in it—Bernard's whiskers, as has been remarked, were much stronger on strength than length—fail to accept such evidence of his true concern for her? She couldn't. Gently stroking the poor uprooted member, she actually bestowed upon it a tear. Bernard hastily folded it in his spotted handkerchief to keep it damp as long as possible, and thus peace and mutual understanding settled over the Kleenex like a refreshing dew and the Air Hostess had no idea of what a tempestuous scene she came in on the end of.

'This time neither the one of you even labelled!' said Miss Fitzpatrick resignedly. 'Very well; you must just shift for yourselves and pick up whatever crumbs going, for I've enough on my hands as it is.—At least you don't require passports,' she added, 'and where on earth I'm to disembark passengers *without* passports I only wish I could ask my Granny!'

Actually Miss Bianca had been struck by the same point; so a couple of hours later, while everyone else was deep in sleep, she slipped from the Hostess's cubicle and made her way to the Oriental Ambassador's V.I.P. reserved seat.

How tired he looked, the poor Oriental Ambassador!— dressed not now in cloth-of-gold but in a rather crumpled linen suit, and with his tie hanging slack from his loosened collar! He hadn't even taken his shoes off; evidently he'd fallen asleep while still trying to read all the papers that spilled from his brief-case over the blanket provided by the Air Line. '*Irrigation*' Miss Bianca saw one headed, and another, '*Agricultural Implements*'. It quite went to her heart to rouse him, but she had to, if she was to spare Willow and the page-boy the disagreeableness of having to spend the rest of their lives airborne.

'Pray forgive me,' said she, as at the brush of her whiskers the Ambassador opened sleep-heavy eyes. 'Only on a matter of extreme urgency would I have disturbed your well-earned repose!'

Half asleep as he was, the Ambassador recognized her.

'That charming face have I not seen before,' he murmured, with a smile, 'peeping from a boy's pocket?'

'Good gracious!' said Miss Bianca, much flattered. 'I didn't intend Your Excellency to notice me!'

'Then it would have been my loss,' the Ambassador

assured her gallantly, 'for to me you provided the grace-note of the whole evening! I only wish I'd known you envisaged a trip to the Orient; I might have had the privilege of escorting you out as well as back.'

Of course in a sense he *had* escorted her out; however the point was too complicated to explain to an Ambassador only half awake. Even as he went on to express a courteous hope that she'd enjoyed herself, it was through a yawn—which Miss Bianca as courteously ignored.

'Quite immensely,' said she. 'Not only was my ambition to stroke a peacock at last fulfilled, but I also rode an elephant. My immediate concern with Your Excellency, however, is to beg Your Excellency to make out a couple of passports in the names of M. (For Madam) Willow, and B. (for Boy) Page.'

Half in a dream, the Ambassador did so.—It was Miss Bianca who found the proper sheets of paper for him, out of his brief-case, also the big official stamp upon which she sat down herself to make the proper official impression. Then she carried the precious documents back with her, and slipped one into the hands of M. Willow and the other into B. Page's sash, where the Air Hostess found them next morning.

'Goodness me!' thought Miss Fitzpatrick. 'So they've passports after all! However did I fail to notice? Now I can at least disembark them at the first stop—which isn't it where you two got on?' she added, to Miss Bianca and Bernard. 'Then you shall all disembark together,' she decided, 'and good luck go with you!'

But first she helped Willow and the page-boy to make themselves clean and tidy, and lent to each one of her own neat overalls, and thus with their passports in their hands they followed the line through the Customs quite easily. To make things easier still, there just outside was Miss Bianca's own Ambassador come to wave a greeting to his colleague, and who, being the kindest man in the world, when he saw two strangers standing obviously nervous and bewildered, took them back in his car to the Embassy to be sorted out. Of course Bernard and Miss Bianca got in too, and making themselves small on the floor sat so close together their whiskers were practically brushing. If he'd still had his longest, Bernard felt, they actually *would* have brushed; but since it was his sacrifice of it that had stopped Miss Bianca being cross with him he didn't regret the circumstance, especially as he had it wrapped in his spotted handkerchief to take out and look at.

What a happy reunion it was, between Miss Bianca and her own Boy in the Embassy schoolroom!—Miss Bianca regaining the Pagoda just in time to welcome him back as in he burst from summer camp scattering fishing-rods, cricket-bats, tennis-racquets and boxing-gloves in every direction! The Boy's first hug was for his mother; then he hugged Miss Bianca almost to suffocation!.

'You haven't been too lonely and bored, Miss Bianca?' he enquired anxiously. 'Next year I'll take you with me! —but I do hope you haven't been *too* bored?'

Miss Bianca but smiled a diplomatic smile!

2

B. Page was adopted as a nephew by the Boy's tutor, who already had one nephew living with him, and kindly said the more the merrier, and all did lessons together.

Willow turned out to be exactly the sort of person needed at the local Orphanage to teach music, embroidery and consideration for others. Under her beneficent influence all the Orphans grew up so charming, they married the moment they were old enough, and so became no longer Orphans—a husband counting as family.

The Captain of the aircraft and Miss Fitzpatrick got married as soon as they had a week's leave together, and lived happy ever after, as did Muslin and Vanilla with the two handsomest boys in Vanilla's uncle's village.

Hathi, now that his eyes were opened, positively refused to do any more trampling, nor, under his leadership, would any of the other elephants, and the cruel custom quite died out.

The silk pavilion in the Pagoda grounds was a great success, especially during that winter, which was exceptionally severe. As Bernard had foreseen, Miss Bianca could sit out of doors in it, catching any sunshine going, and remain perfectly warm and snug; and Bernard often shared the privilege, talking about polo. A particularly delightful circumstance was that this very spot, or pouch, in which the whole adventure began, proved to have been embroidered by Willow herself!

The faithless Ali was never seen again. Sometimes the conservatory gardener fancied he glimpsed the tip of a green tail, but it was always a curling tendril, or swaying stem, or drooping fern frond; and whether the Ambassadorial conservatory still has a snakeling in it is unknown to this day.

BERNARD THE BRAVE

Illustrated by Faith Jaques

To Geoffrey Castle

I

HOW IT ALL BEGAN

IT MAY BE remembered that at the end of *Miss Bianca and the Bridesmaid* the author said that was the very last tale of Bernard and Miss Bianca and the Mouse Prisoners' Aid Society, and so it was. *This* story is about Bernard on his own, for surely his unexampled bravery deserves a book to itself.

Bernard had no idea he was going to be so exceptionally brave. It just happened, soon after Miss Bianca told him she was going to be away for three weeks.

They had been sitting together, as they always did between five and seven in the evening, in the little pleasure-ground surrounding Miss Bianca's Porcelain Pagoda. 'Twas a charming spot indeed, with gay flower-beds bordering a Venetian glass fountain, swing seats to sit on, and for recreation a little light see-saw. A few Japanese parasols, of the sort stuck into ices, merely added colour, for since the whole desirable property was situated in the Embassy schoolroom, there was never any fear of too much sun or a passing shower. The schoolroom was where the Boy, the Ambassador's son, did his lessons—and how many happy, useful hours had Miss Bianca passed there,

sitting on his shoulder to help him with his geography or
history or mathematics! Not even his tutor objected to her
presence, after the Boy's mother, the Ambassadress, had
explained that Miss Bianca was quite a friend of the
family! For the Ambassadress knew nothing of Miss
Bianca's hair-raising extra-curricular activities in connec-
tion with the M.P.A.S.: to her Miss Bianca was just an
exceptionally intelligent and charming white mouse.
—Charming indeed was Miss Bianca, with her silvery fur
and huge brown eyes! The eyes of most white mice are
pink; Miss Bianca's were the colour of topaz, and fringed
by long dark lashes. Bernard was never tired of looking at
her; beauty always appeals particularly to the plain, and it
must be admitted that Bernard himself was plain as a boot,
though very powerfully built and with particularly strong,
though short and stubby, whiskers. He would have been
quite content just to sit there in the garden looking at Miss
Bianca all evening; only she had something on her mind.

For not for several weeks now had the Boy done any
lessons. He'd had mumps with complications, and the very
next day was to be taken to convalesce in the bracing air
of a winter resort in the mountains, and it was this news
Miss Bianca had to break.

'My dear Bernard,' said she, interrupting the compan-
ionable silence, 'you know the Boy is well on the road to
recovery?'

'Good-oh,' said Bernard. 'I remember you telling me he
had mumps.'

'And is now to be taken,' continued Miss Bianca, 'to
convalesce in the bracing air of a mountain resort.'

'Very sensible,' said Bernard. 'One of my nephews—
would it be young Nibbler?—didn't properly get over the
mumps before catching measles.' (No wonder he couldn't
remember the name; he had seventy nephews and nieces.)
'How long is the Boy going for?'

'Three weeks,' said Miss Bianca, 'and I'm very much
afraid, dear Bernard, that I shall be away for the same
length of time. We leave tomorrow morning.'

It was a few moments before this information sank in to
Bernard's then agitated breast.

'Away for three *weeks*?' he exclaimed. 'Why, Miss Bianca, that's ages and ages!' (So three weeks were, to a mouse.) 'Why on earth must you go as well?'

'The Boy happens to be rather attached to me,' said Miss Bianca modestly.

'As well he may,' snorted Bernard, 'but he'll have all that bracing air to console him. What about me, left behind with no more than a whiff from the cheese-factory? I shall come too,' declared Bernard. 'I know *you* always travel in the Boy's pocket, but if I have to hitch-hike I'll make it. I've never seen a mountain,' he added. 'We could look at one together, Miss Bianca!'

Miss Bianca sighed. Fond as she was of her old comrade, and thoroughly as she appreciated his sterling qualities, she felt she was going to have her hands quite full enough without looking at mountains with Bernard.

'Actually I'd relied on your watering my garden for me,' said she.

Though it was November, owing to the practically hot-house conditions in the schoolroom, Miss Bianca's flowers bloomed all the year round, but of course needed a great deal of watering.

'Albert Footman will see to that,' said Bernard.

'Actually since Albert Footman has been courting one of the chambermaids,' said Miss Bianca, for once rather censoriously, 'he's little better than a broken reed.—My poor daisies! There's a little pink one just coming out.'

Bernard paused a moment. Then—

'You mean you'd rather I stayed behind to water your daisies?' he asked.

'To be frank, yes,' said Miss Bianca. ''Twould be the greatest comfort to me!'

Since anything that would be a comfort to Miss Bianca was okay with Bernard, he, however reluctantly, gave up his plans to hitch-hike and promised to stay behind on the job.

He little guessed that when Miss Bianca came back her garden would be dry as a bone!

Next morning off the big Rolls Royce rolled bearing the Boy and his mother to their mountain resort. (The Ambassador couldn't go with them owing to his ambassadorial duties.) The Ambassadress saw her son slip Miss Bianca into his pocket, but only smiled. As has been said, she was very fond of Miss Bianca herself—it was she who'd given Miss Bianca the silver chain she always wore round her neck—and also realized that to be parted from his best friend might well set back the Boy's convalescence. However, since the Boy's pocket already contained two fish hooks and a lump of toffee, Miss Bianca was out again as soon as in, and he had to turn his pocket quite out before she could travel in reasonable comfort. Then off the car rolled bearing the Boy and his mother and Miss Bianca to the bracing airs of the mountain resort, leaving Bernard behind.

He couldn't even wave goodbye. There were too many footmen about, helping put the luggage in. The car rolled off, and Bernard was left alone.

'It's only for three weeks,' he told himself bravely. 'I'll

have time to get my stamp album in proper order . . .'

It was only for three weeks. The mornings were all right: first he went and watered the Pagoda garden, also cleaned out (turning the tap off first) the Venetian glass fountain. Then there was all the M.P.A.S. correspondence to see to—for he was still its Secretary, though Miss Bianca had long retired from being its Madam Chairwoman—and after lunch his stamp album to occupy him. But between five and seven he simply didn't know what to do with himself.

Some of his neighbours in the cigar-cabinet where he had a flat invited him to wine-and-cheese parties.—Since

the Ambassador stopped smoking, his cigar-cabinet was
one of the best mouse addresses going; one of Bernard's
neighbours was a fashionable doctor, one a fashionable
optician, one a chartered accountant; wine-and-cheese
parties were part of their way of life, there was one almost
every evening. But Bernard soon found them if anything
a bore—the conversation so regularly turned on the wonderful adventures he'd shared with Miss Bianca. Not that
the *object* of these adventures, the rescuing of prisoners,
much interested such sophisticated, worldling mice; to
their discredit, none was even a member of the M.P.A.S.;
they just wanted to hear about the celebrated Miss Bianca!

'Tell us more about Miss Bianca in the Black Castle!'
begged Bernard's neighbours. 'How wonderfully brave
she must have been, to face that terrible cat!'

'Actually it was me he had actually in his clutches,' said
Bernard.

'Really?—But tell us about Miss Bianca in the Diamond
Palace!' pressed Bernard's neighbours. 'Wasn't it quite
heroic of her to face those mechanical ladies-in-waiting?'

'Actually it was me, disguised as a knife-grinder, who
finally pulled off the rescue,' said Bernard—but no one
seemed to want to hear about *his* heroism at all!

Thus a rather sore and unhappy mouse was Bernard ere
Miss Bianca had been gone but a week. Stumping gloomily
back to his own flat after a wine-and-cheese party, he
slammed the door and put 'Out' on it and resolved not to
open it again (except of course for the laundry and milk

and to go and water Miss Bianca's garden), and lead a hermit's life until she came back.

As the first step towards becoming a hermit he went straight to bed, and having rather drowned his sorrows at the wine part of the wine-and-cheese party, went straight to sleep. How long he slept he didn't know, but it must have been in the small hours of the morning that he was aroused by a loud, repeated knocking on his with-'Out'-on-it front door.

'Botheration!' thought Bernard. 'Whoever it is can just go *on* knocking!'

But it was more than a knocking, it was a positive battering—enough to wake all the neighbours, Also it didn't stop.

'At least I'll give whoever it is a piece of my mind!' thought Bernard, as he got grumpily out of bed and opened up.

There on the threshold stood a mouse so aged and decrepit (actually on crutches), so apparently incapable of kicking up such a row on his own, Bernard instinctively looked past him to see if there wasn't a gang of young Hallowe'en rowdies with him. But no; he was alone; and Bernard realized that what he'd been banging on the door with must have been a crutch, used practically as a battering-ram.

'You've been long enough answering,' complained the old mouse, 'when there isn't a moment to lose! You *are* Bernard?'

'If you mean, am I the Permanent Secretary of the M.P.A.S.,' answered Bernard stiffly, 'I am. And I think you might have better manners than to come banging on my door when you see "Out" on it. However, since you seem to know my name, what can I do for you?'

'I don't suppose *you* can do anything,' said the old mouse. 'Lead me to Miss Bianca!'

'I'm afraid she's away,' said Bernard, more stiffly still, 'enjoying the bracing air of a mountain resort.'

'Away? How long for?' panted the old mouse.

'Three weeks,' said Bernard. 'Actually, now, two weeks minus a day.'

'Then it may be too late!' cried the old mouse; and stumbling in before Bernard could stop him, he collapsed into Bernard's best armchair with his crutches on the floor beside it.

'Well, as you're here, I suppose you may as well get whatever it is off your chest,' said Bernard resignedly.

2

NICODEMUS'S TALE

'MY NAME,' OPENED the old mouse, now more calmly, 'is Nicodemus; nor have I always been as you now see me.'

'Well, I should hope not,' said Bernard, 'because to me, if I may say so, you look a perfect wreck.'

'Believe it or not, in my youth I was a Waltzing Mouse,' said Nicodemus, 'excelling above all in the Viennese variety. It was for that particular skill my young mistress induced her guardian—for she was left orphaned at an early age—to purchase me off an itinerant showman. Ah me, what a happy life I then led, performing not for ignorant rustics but for a young lady with a thorough knowledge of music! Naturally time passed; I grew older; I grew even arthritic; but did my dear Miss Tomasina ever chide me? No. She made me these crutches with her own hands!'

'Not a bad job of work,' said Bernard, surveying them rather critically, 'though I dare say any one of our joiners would have done better. If you want her name inscribed in the M.P.A.S. Records Book, I assure you I can see to it just as well as Miss Bianca.'

'But only Miss Bianca can *rescue* her!' cried Nicodemus.

For a moment, in renewed agitation, he started up from Bernard's best armchair with such sudden feverish energy, Bernard was afraid he was going to have a fit; and with a soothing (also firm) hand shoved him back.

'Rescue her who from?' asked Bernard.

'Her guardian would tell you, from bandits,' said Nicodemus, somewhat controlling himself, 'who seized her while walking in the woods. Her guardian would tell you 'tis bandits who have stolen her away—for how else account for her disappearance? But in my belief 'tis he himself who has caused her to vanish—on the very eve of her eighteenth birthday when she comes of age, in order to claim all her rich heritage for his own! For unless she's there to claim it herself before the Board of Estates, all falls into his hands!'

Bernard went over to the sideboard and poured out two glasses of elderberry cordial. Elderberry cordial always helped to clear his mind, and the laws of hospitality forbade him to drink alone.

'I take it that besides being an orphan she's an heiress?' he checked.

'To lands and villages without number!' cried Nicodemus. 'To the whole Three Rivers Estate!'

In an instant all Bernard's budding sympathy vanished. The shocking conditions at Three Rivers were notorious even in the city a hundred miles away. Never was a peasantry more downtrodden and abused—compelled to do forced labour, evicted from their homes, their commons stolen away from them!

'The Three Rivers?' he repeated vigorously. 'Then I'm

not surprised she's disappeared; I'm only surprised she
hasn't been lynched!'

'No, no!' cried Nicodemus. 'Though the conditions
(as you are obviously aware) are deplorable indeed, Miss
Tomasina knows nothing of them! Her guardian treats
her like a child—and a child she still is—only *nearly*
eighteen! When she rides or walks out, 'tis never beyond
the Park gates or into the home woods: she sees nothing to
displease her eye or arouse her suspicions. *She* has the
tenderest heart in the world—didn't she make my crutches
with her own hands?—and in my belief 'tis partly for that
very reason, because she isn't cruel and ruthless as himself,
and would never be a party to his evil ways, that her
wicked guardian has had her made off with!'

Of course this altered the whole complexion of things,
and Bernard's sympathies started to revive again.

'I'll tell you how tender-hearted she is!' went on
Nicodemus, more and more eagerly. 'Once, walking in
the home woods and coming upon a tree-feller who'd had
an accident with his axe, she bound up the wound with her
own petticoat which within a week his wife sent back
laundered with a bunch of flowers for their dear young
lady!'

The recollection was too much for him and he burst
into sobs. Great tears started to his eyes and rolled down his
shabby whiskers; he wiped them away with his fists—
evidently he didn't possess a handkerchief—but still they
flowed, while Bernard's sympathies revived more and
more. However he kept a cool head, though in it a daring
plan was already beginning to form.

'Well, if she *hasn't* been kidnapped by bandits,' enquired Bernard, 'where do you suppose she is?'

'Why, in the attic of her guardian's town house in this very city!' gulped Nicodemus. 'Where else can he be so sure of obedient servants carrying up meals to an imprisoned young lady?—until they perhaps stop carrying up meals at all! Oh, Miss Bianca, how I need you!'

Bernard came to a rapid decision.

'Since Miss Bianca isn't available,' said he, 'I'll have a shot at rescuing your young lady myself.'

Bernard was never in the least jealous of Miss Bianca's fame, but he did for once want to do a rescue off his own bat!

'*You* will?' exclaimed Nicodemus incredulously—yet with rising hope.

'Yes, me,' said Bernard. 'I've had more experience in prisoner-rescuing than you seem to realize. I don't suppose a few hours will make any difference; you doss down where you are and I'll go back to bed.'

For he always believed in getting a good night's rest before any unusual enterprise, and if possible a good breakfast as well.

However after such a broken night both he and Nicodemus slept most of the next day; and it was rather a high tea (of cheese parings, bacon rinds and piccalilli) that they eventually sat down to.

'You said last night,' checked Bernard, 'that Miss Tomasina is probably incarcerated in her guardian's town house here in the city. What's the exact address?'

'That I can't tell you,' said Nicodemus. 'All our lives we've lived outside town, a hundred miles off. (If you ask how I got here, it was by way of a farmer's waggon delivering eggs to the General Store.) But what I do know is, it's the biggest house on the Grand Boulevard.'

Bernard was impressed. All the houses on the Grand Boulevard were big—one was actually a Young Ladies' Boarding School, and one, when it was torn down, made space for a supermarket—so the biggest must be a stately edifice indeed, practically a palace, and Bernard had always had a mistrust of palaces ever since his and Miss Bianca's dreadful experiences in the Ranee's palace in the Orient. However, he let none of his misgivings appear.

'Then somehow or other I'll get into it,' said he, 'and if I find Miss Tomasina there, speak a few reassuring words to her and then—'

'Summon the Police!' cried Nicodemus. 'My word, won't they be mad, when they're probably hunting bandits all over the place this very minute! And my word won't they take it out of her guardian, for setting them on a false trail! Hard labour won't be good enough for him, whilst I'll personally belabour him with my crutch!'

So saying, he reached for one of the crutches lying beside him and attempted to swing it in the air.—The effort proved too much; his arthritis caught up with him, and he absolutely collapsed with his whiskers in the piccalilli.

'You've done all that could be expected of you already,' said Bernard kindly. 'You need rest. Just leave the whole operation to me.'

For not only did he see Nicodemus, with his crutches and arthritis, as a clog in the enterprise, he also very much wished to pull off a rescue on his own. Putting on his new long-distance glasses, and taking his mackintosh from its peg—

'Leave the whole operation to me!' repeated Bernard, and strode out into the gathering dusk.

3

THE BIGGEST HOUSE ON THE GRAND BOULEVARD

IT WAS JUST as well he'd taken his mackintosh, for the winter evening was cold and drizzly—in fact the drizzle soon turned into a fine but penetrating rain. Bernard was actually rather glad of it, as he turned up his collar and hurried on, for it kept people (and cats) indoors, and he didn't wish to attract notice. The only disadvantage was that the raindrops so blurred his glasses, he had to keep taking them off and wiping them, and even so had but a foggy view of each enormous house. He could tell the supermarket all right, from its huge plate glass windows stuffed with breakfast foods and tinned salmon; otherwise, from mouse-level, each house on the Grand Boulevard looked as big as the next. Bernard had to judge simply by the width of their doorsteps; but one doorstep was so unmistakably widest of all, up he confidently nipped.

Then what met his view? The lower panels of a great, shut, oaken door—just like the door of a prison!

'This is where Miss Tomasina is incarcerated all right!' thought Bernard, 'but how on earth do I get in?'

His experience of prisons however had taught him that

however rebarbative their frontage, there was often a
weakness at the back; so down he ran again and nosed
cautiously round the building's huge bulk, where his
expectations were fulfilled by the sight of several over-
flowing dustbins outside a smaller, more homely entrance.
In fact the dustbins so overflowed and the back door was so
jammed ajar by cartons and waste-paper, Bernard was
easily able to slip in.

First into a cellar, then into a boiler-room. So loudly
roared the incinerator in the boiler-room, Bernard skirted
it respectfully; and perceived behind it another door ajar,
opening onto a narrow staircase.

'Twas a toilsome climb indeed he had to undertake, for
the stone steps, though worn, were still steep, and Bernard
thought regretfully of the service-lifts at the Embassy. 'If
it's as tough going all the way up to the attics,' thought
Bernard, 'I shall be too breathless to speak even *one*
reassuring word to Miss Tomasina!' As the staircase, on
the first landing, passed a green baize door on the other side
of which (he could tell by the smells) was obviously the
kitchen, where there probably *would* be a service-lift,
Bernard was very much tempted to slip in and chance his
luck. But he knew how heavy-handed cooks could be, at
the sight of a mouse, and prudently resigned himself to
continuing upward toil.

Up toiled Bernard past a second green baize door, and
when he came to a third, felt he must surely have
reached the attics at last. Pausing only to wipe his
spectacles Bernard pushed through it and entered —

Obviously *not* an attic!

It was one of the biggest rooms Bernard had ever seen. It was bigger than the Ambassadress's drawing-room. But a drawing-room it certainly wasn't either. It contained twenty little white beds, neatly ranged in two rows of ten, with beside each a locker or play-box, and upon each a little white nightgown neatly folded . . .

It took several moments to realize the truth. For the first moment he just thought that Miss Tomasina's wicked guardian must have an exceptionally fine family: families of twenty are nothing to a mouse. Then he recalled that human families are usually limited to five or six at the most, and then of varying ages; twenty little daughters all the *same* age (by the size of their beds and nightgowns), were surely beyond the power of human reproduction . . .

Also Nicodemus had said nothing of Miss Tomasina's guardian being even married . . .

At last light dawned: it wasn't Miss Tomasina's guardian's town house he'd penetrated with such pains, but the Boarding School for Young Ladies!

And just as light *did* dawn, in scampered twenty little girls come to tidy themselves up before supper!

To Bernard there seemed at least forty of them, as they ran in giggling and squealing and enjoying a brief interval of release from under the eyes of their teachers. Some were blonde, some brunette, one carroty; some had their hair in pigtails, some in ringlets, some in fringes; but my

goodness how they all giggled and squealed! Bernard's
wits were quite bemused, and instead of making for cover
he stood where he was, obvious to every eye, in the middle
of the floor.

And did the Young Ladies show any fear of him? Not
they. (It may be remembered that Miss Bianca, attacking
the Diamond Castle to rescue a little girl called Patience,
had based her entire strategy on the hypothesis that the
Diamond Duchess's ladies-in-waiting, at first sight of a
mouse, would immediately jump on chairs.) But the
Young Ladies were made of sterner stuff. (Some of their
brothers kept ferrets.) They clustered round Bernard with
cries of positive enthusiasm!

'Why, look, here's a mouse!' cried all the little girls—
apparently quite unaware that if they'd had any true
feminine sensibility they should have been jumping on
chairs. (Actually there weren't any chairs in the dormitory,
but they could have jumped on their beds.) 'Oh, isn't he
cute!' cried all the little girls. 'Isn't he cunning?'

They pressed so close, Bernard was absolutely hemmed
in by plimsolls; and since in any unusual circumstances it
is always best to stick to conventions, he took two steps
back, then one forward and pulled his whiskers.

'Why, look, he's been *trained*!' cried all the little girls.
'Oh, isn't he a darling? Isn't he a perfect pet?' (Bernard
had never felt such a fool in his life.) 'Why, let's *keep* him
for a pet!'

'But we aren't allowed pets,' said a prim looking girl
in pigtails. 'If Headmistress found him—'

'Then she mustn't!' cried Carrotty. 'Don't be such a

spoilsport! *I* know where we'll keep him—in my play-box! It's got holes in the lid where my brother tried out an electric drill and nothing inside but an old teddy bear! We'll put him in my box and feed him cheese from our suppers, and take him out to play with in the dormitory here at night!'

This brilliant plan was at once agreed to, and within moments Bernard found himself popped into one of the big wooden boxes and heard the lid slammed down; and then after hastily tidying themselves, all the Young Ladies ran off giggling.

'Here's a pretty kettle of sardine-tails!' thought Bernard grimly.

For though he pushed with all his might, he couldn't raise the heavy wooden lid by so much as a half-inch, and the holes bored by Carrotty's brother weren't big enough for even a mouse to squeeze through . . .

It was true he might have been worse off. At least he wasn't going to suffocate, nor was he likely to starve, if the little girls remembered to bring back enough cheese; but small consolation was either circumstance to Bernard, set out to rescue an imprisoned young lady and now a prisoner himself!

Meanwhile Miss Bianca for her part wasn't finding her hands nearly so full as she'd expected. The mountain resort where the Ambassadress had taken a villa, or chalet, was one of the most beautiful spots imaginable: high snow-covered peaks surrounded a wide smooth lake that reflected the blue of a perpetually cloudless sky, the fir trees, under their load of melting ice—for the sun, after each frosty night, shone punctually all day—looked like Christmas trees; as for the bracingness of the air, it was so remarkably bracing that the Boy quite recovered almost as soon as he got there, and had no need of Miss Bianca to keep him amused!

There was naturally no bathing in the lake, but there was water-skiing on it, just as there was proper skiing on the mountain slopes, and the Boy, as he grew stronger and stronger, began to take part in both these sports. He also began to make friends with other children whose parents had taken chalets round about, and the Ambassadress was pleased to see it, for thoroughly as she appreciated Miss Bianca's qualities, she sometimes felt a white mouse not quite adequate as her son's best friend, and was glad to see him in the company of other boys and girls—as the Boy soon came to be from the moment he finished breakfast till he was (reluctantly) put to bed.

There were other amusements too, at the mountain resort. Sometimes one of the big hotels put on a concert, or a fancy dress dance; once a whole travelling circus briefly pitched its tents—and then what excitement! Besides the circus proper there were all sorts of sideshows; in one an old lady told fortunes, in another a mustachioed old man and a lad played on hurdy-gurdies to accompany a pair of waltzing mice! The Boy nearly fetched Miss Bianca to see them; then he reflected that the sight might upset her, the poor mice looked so tired!

For of course the Boy didn't actually *neglect* Miss Bianca. As soon as they got to the chalet he made a very nice nest for her in a drawer lined with clean handkerchiefs, and never forgot to change them. He also took her for a promenade each morning on the window-sill, brought her up cheese and biscuits after lunch, and before going to sleep always saw that besides his own glass of water by the bed there was a little saucer-full for Miss Bianca in case she was thirsty in the night. The Ambassadress kept an eye on her too, and often looked in to report the Boy's progress towards complete recovery. But the fact remained that Miss Bianca was bored stiff.

As usual, she found a resource in poetry—but the poem she wrote after a week at the mountain resort was quite unlike her usual sort of verse!

UNUSUAL POEM WRITTEN BY MISS BIANCA
WHILE STAYING AT A MOUNTAIN RESORT
'Without, how white the snow, how blue the sky!
  Blue too the lake that ripples to the shore!
All nature smiles!—Alas, ungrateful I
  To wish for something more!

Without, the moon in beauty rides on high,
  Bright frosty starlets twinkle by the score!
All nature dreams in bliss!—Ungrateful I
  To find all nature just one great big bore!'

M.B.

When Miss Bianca re-read the poem she tore it up. But it had undoubtedly been expressive of her feelings at the time.

Also expressive of her feelings was another, shorter poem written by Miss Bianca a little later.

SHORTER POEM WRITTEN BY MISS BIANCA
'O Bernard, are you quite well?
  O Bernard, are you all right?
    You will water my garden I know,
    I shall find every flower a-blow,
  But are you quite well and all right,
  Out of my sight?'

M.B.

How Bernard would have rejoiced to read those simple but heartfelt lines, proving that Miss Bianca really cared for him!

Of course he was quite *well*, but by no stretch of the imagination could he have been called *all right*—imprisoned as he was, at the very moment when Miss Bianca set pen to paper, in a locker in the dormitory of a Young Ladies' Boarding School!

4

ALGERNON

BERNARD PUSHED AND pushed against the heavy wooden lid until every muscle ached. Then he tried nibbling round an air hole in the hopes of enlarging it sufficiently for him to be able to squeeze through. But the play-box was made of teak, the hardest wood there is, and he soon realized that his teeth would be worn to stumps before he achieved any success. Frustrated and exhausted, Bernard at last quite collapsed—but at least onto something soft . . .

It was Carrotty's teddy bear. As teddy bears go it was quite a small one, little more than eight inches or so long, with gingery fur and boot-button eyes, and a general air of dilapidation only to be expected after a life with Carrotty!

'Pardon me,' said Bernard—ever polite though practically *in extremis*. 'I was so bent on trying to get out I didn't notice you.' Then he clutched so to speak at a straw, of which several protruded through the bear's worn gingery coat. 'I suppose *you* couldn't shove a bit too?' suggested Bernard.

'Aw'fly sowwy, old chap,' lisped the teddy bear (who

came originally from a great London toy shop), 'but I've lost so much of my stuffing, I'm perfectly incapable of any effort whatever!'

'But this is a matter of urgency,' pressed Bernard. 'I've absolutely got to get out of here without loss of time in order to rescue a young lady held prisoner by her wicked guardian.'

'Goodness me, what an exciting life you must lead!' admired the teddy bear. 'You don't play polo too, by any chance?'

'Actually I have,' said Bernard. 'With an Indian team called the Princely Orchids.'

'Dashed sporting chaps, some of those Indians,' said the teddy bear. 'Dashed good at cwicket too. My name's Algernon, if it's of any intewest.'

'Mine's Bernard,' said Bernard. 'I'm also—if it's of any interest—Secretary of the Mouse Prisoners' Aid Society; so you'll see why I have to get on with the job.'

'You seem to be a dashed sporting chap all wound,' complimented Algernon. 'All wight, I'll do my feeble best!'

His best wasn't so bad after all; his stuffing wasn't quite all out of him. Bernard's and Algernon's united efforts raised the lid just sufficiently for Bernard to squeeze out—and looking back, he saw that Algernon, by inserting his muzzle (stuffed with wood shavings), had shoved it actually high enough for him to scramble out too.

'I've got so dashed bored here,' he explained, 'I believe I'll come along with you on your pwisoner wescuing!'

Bernard had first got himself into a Young Ladies'

Boarding School, then he'd been called cute. Now the last thing he wanted was an effete soft toy tagging after him.

'Don't think of it,' said Bernard hastily. 'Much as I appweciate'—Algernon's lisp was catching—'your gallant offer, far better stay where you are!'

But Algernon was already flexing long-disused muscles.

'One of my long-ago ancestors,' he remarked, 'was I believe spared from being shot by the Amewican Pwesident Teddy Woosevelt—hence our family nickname.

How I wish he'd been spared from being shot by George Washington! However the nickname, as I say, has tagged us ever since, and I must say I'd like to add a little lustre to it. Which way do we go now?'

'Obviously first down to street level,' said Bernard resignedly—also rather deliberately rolling the 'r' in street—'to start again; for it seems Miss Tomasina isn't incarcerated here at all. So down again it must be, and I hope you can show me where we get on to the service-lift because I've had enough of stairs, up *or* down, to last me a lifetime.'

'It's easy to see you know little about boarding schools,' said Algernon. 'The only service-lift *here* wuns non-stop between the kitchen and the Headmistwess's own quarters; all the spoiled papers the young ladies have done exercises on in class, like all the Kleenex and curl-papers they leave lying about in the dormitory, are collected in sacks by scwubwomen and taken down to the back door by hand. Actually Addie and Amy should be here in two shakes—which may be a bit of luck for you and me!'

'You mean our best chance of getting down is in a scrub-woman's sack?' demanded Bernard distastefully.

'Our *only* chance,' corrected Algernon. 'Hark, here they come! Lie low and pwetend to be dead, like me!'

It was easy enough for Algernon to pretend he was dead. He just *un*flexed his muscles and let himself flop—flat as though he'd been run over. But Bernard was in the pink of condition—(if a little overweight; he weighed an ounce and a half)—moreover after all his efforts he was still puffing like a miniature steam engine. However by lying supine with all four feet in the air he trusted to deceive a scrubwoman's passing glance.

And so he did; for scarcely had Addie and Amy entered and begun their work than the latter let out a squeal quite unlike the pleased squeals of the little girls.

'Goodness, here's a dead mouse!' cried she. 'Do put it in *your* sack, dear, for I never could abide mice dead or alive!'

'You're too sensitive for your own good, dear,' said Addie, boldly picking up Bernard by the tail and tossing him in among the spoiled exercise papers. 'And here's an old teddy bear!' she added. 'What rubbish the young ladies do turn out of their lockers!'

So in went Algernon beside Bernard; and the two scrub-women, after collecting all the Kleenexes and curl-papers as well, set off downstairs—chatting all the way.

On the first floor down (against a clatter, through the baize door, of the young ladies' knives and forks at supper), they just discussed their Easter bonnets—Easter bonnets meaning as much to a scrubwoman as any topknot worn by a *midinette* in Paris on St. Catherine's Day. But on the second, where the empty classrooms were, Amy thought of something else.

'—with blue velvet ribbons and a pink rose. My good-ness, I've just remembered!' she exclaimed.

'That I'm having a pink rose on mine?' said Addie.

'No, dear—though now you mention it, didn't *I* choose a pink rose first? What I've only just now remembered is that all the dustmen are on strike. So it's no use putting *this* lot outside to be collected, 'twill only mean more mess and litter round the back door!'

'Aren't you the clever one!' admired Addie. 'What *shall* we do with them, then?'

'Why, pop 'em into the incinerator!' said Amy.

The ears of Bernard and Algernon both burned and froze!

'Look here—' muttered Bernard.

'Just what I was going to say myself,' agreed Algernon.

'We must somehow get out of here before we're, well, burnt to cinders . . .'

'Obviously,' said Algernon. 'As to *how*, I leave entirely to you, old chap!'

By now they had reached the cellarage. Nothing could be heard from above at all—no clatter of knives and forks from the dining-room, no rumour from the kitchen. The only sound that broke the silence was the roaring of the huge, grim, iron-bound incinerator . . .

But did Bernard fail his companion? No. Thrusting up through the Kleenexes and curl-papers he pushed his head out of the sack and yelled Yah-boo!

He hadn't yelled Yah-boo since the how long ago Hallowe'ens when but a stripling mouse he'd followed in his bigger brothers' footsteps demanding tricks or treats!

'Yah-boo!' yelled Bernard again.

'My goodness, it's *alive*!' cried both the scrubwomen together—and (unlike the young ladies) they immediately looked about for something to jump on.—Their only resource was a chopping-block, left over from the days

when the incinerator burned wood, and on it both huddled precariously as Bernard finally scrambled out of the
sack hauling Algernon after him.

'There's a door open behind us,' gasped Bernard. 'Come
quick—Yah-boo!—and we can get away!'

Algernon followed with for an effete soft toy an un-
common turn of speed, also with a cry of Yah-boo on his
own account, and in two shakes they were out in the
kindly shadow of the dust-bins while the incinerator
defrauded of its prey roared more angrily than ever!

'Well, that danger's past!' panted Bernard.

'I'm still not sure why you wanted to get into the Young Ladies' Boarding School at all,' said Algernon, shaking a curl-paper out of his ear.

'I made a bloomer,' said Bernard honestly. 'I took it for the biggest house on the Grand Boulevard, which evidently it isn't. It's these dashed long-distance glasses of mine,' he added. 'I knew at the time I shouldn't have let myself be talked into buying them, and I'll never wear them again! Now we'll just have to *ask* someone which is the biggest . . .'

At that very moment there scurried into view a respectable looking mouse who by the size of the basket she carried was taking home laundry.

'Pardon me, ma'am,' said Bernard, 'but perhaps *you* can tell us which is the biggest house on the Grand Boulevard?'

'Why, the one you've just come out of!' said the washerwoman. 'There *was* a bigger—belonging to a gentleman one heard say living in the country—but he sold it to be torn down to make a site for the supermarket. And I'm sure every mouse should be grateful to him, for the pickings from a supermarket after all the lady cashiers have gone home, are a rodent's dream!'

'Thank you very much,' said Bernard.

'Not at all,' said the washerwoman. 'Only glad to be of service. And if ever you should want any clear-starching, the name is Mrs Nibblecheese.'

With that she hurried on; and there was a slight pause, while it began to rain really hard.

'Where do we go now?' asked Algernon.

'Back home,' said Bernard, 'where I *shall* give Nicodemus a piece of my mind . . .'

5

A FRESH START

IT DIDN'T DO anything to assuage Bernard's wrath that when they arrived at the cigar-cabinet he found that Nicodemus had got at the elderberry cordial again. Not only was the bottle Bernard had poured from the night before quite empty, but Nicodemus had evidently looked into the sideboard for another, and the level in that was pretty far down!

'Well?' he cried eagerly, before Bernard had time to speak. 'Have you found her?'

'No,' said Bernard, taking off his mackintosh.

'You haven't? Then what on earth have you been doing, away all this time?' demanded Nicodemus.

'Thanks to you, making a fool of myself,' said Bernard grimly. 'By the way, that's Algernon outside the front door,'—though small for a teddy bear, Algernon was still too big to get into Bernard's flat—'who has been of the greatest assistance to me, and who I dare say would like a little of that elderberry cordial, as indeed I should myself.'

Just as though it were his own property, Nicodemus tilted the bottle to see how much was left before pushing it across the table.

'Then all I can say,' he snapped, 'is that you're no more good at prisoner-rescuing than my crutch. Oh Miss Bianca—'

'And all *I* can say,' snapped back Bernard, 'is in the first place pipe down about Miss Bianca, and in the second you're a muddle-headed old fool.' (Here he paused to pass Algernon on the landing a glass of elderberry cordial. He also left the front door ajar so that Algernon could hear what was going on. He felt the bear deserved it.) 'Miss Tomasina's guardian's town house,' he continued, 'has been pulled down to make room for a supermarket, and the biggest house on the Grand Boulevard happens to be now,' said Bernard bitterly, 'a Young Ladies' Boarding School. You seem to know so little about what's been going on, I begin to doubt whether Miss Tomasina has really disappeared at all.'

'But she has!' cried Nicodemus. 'Indeed, indeed she has! I may have jumped to a wrong conclusion—knowing nothing about her guardian's dealings in real estate—but indeed, indeed she's vanished! One day playing waltzes on the piano, the next totally disappeared—and within but weeks of her birthday! Pray forgive my thoughtless reference to Miss Bianca, and go on undertaking the search yourself!'

'Certainly I shall,' said Bernard, 'though probably only to find she's visiting friends or relations . . .'

'But she has no friends or relations!' cried Nicodemus. 'Never was a poor rich heiress so alone in all the world! Perhaps 'tis bandits after all who have kidnapped her—but bribed to do so by her wicked guardian!'

'What's your opinion?' asked Bernard of Algernon through the door.

'All bandits being by definition bad hats,' replied Algernon judiciously, 'and most guardians as well, I'd say it's highly pwobable. Only where do you suppose they've got her?'

'Somewhere in the mountains, of course,' said Bernard.

For it was common knowledge that all bandits lived in the mountains, whence they descended to make raids on the peaceful citizenry—and even as he spoke Bernard's

heart gave a leap, because anywhere in the mountains he'd
be at least *nearer* to Miss Bianca, and might even encounter
her at her bracing resort!

'Only don't they cover a goodish awea?' asked
Algernon.

'Indeed they do,' said Bernard, 'and this is where we've
got to get some sense out of our friend here.—Now then,'
he addressed Nicodemus, 'where do the Three Rivers
your estate's named after flow down from?'

'Why, the great Wolf Range!' said Nicodemus.

Bernard's heart stopped leaping and thumped. The
Wolf Range was the highest, and barrenest, and altogether
most fearsome part of the mountains, and it was quite
unthinkable that anyone should have built a resort there.
Regretfully, he put all thoughts of meeting Miss Bianca
aside, and at the same moment remembered something.

'Look here,' remembered Bernard, 'didn't you say the
Police were hunting bandits all over the place already, and
how mad they'd be with Miss Tomasina's guardian for
putting them on the wrong track? Now it seems he
didn't put them on the wrong track; so why haven't they
found her?'

'I see you have a better opinion of our Police than is
common,' said Nicodemus. 'I dare say a few might search
about the foot-hills, but not one would go up into the
Wolf Range!'

('They can't be much like our London Bobbies,' put in
Algernon. 'A London Bobby would go up Alps, in the
course of duty!')

'So most probably it *is* into the Wolf Range Miss

Tomasina has been kidnapped,' said Bernard, 'and into the Wolf Range I shall penetrate tomorrow morning.—No you don't,' he added, as Nicodemus reached for the cordial bottle again (possibly to drink a toast to Bernard's heroic resolve?). 'You just think of anything else useful you can remember, for instance, whether Miss Tomasina has anything to recognize her by—such as a mole on the left cheek.'

'How extraordinary you should ask!' exclaimed Nicodemus. 'Actually she *has* a mole on her cheek—though not on the left, on the right. We used to call it her beauty-spot . . .'

'At least that's some means of identification,' said Bernard. 'Algernon,' he went on, through the front door, 'I shall be leaving tomorrow for the Wolf Range, and how you're to get back to your play-box I'm afraid I don't know.'

'I don't either,' said Algernon, 'but it doesn't matter. I'll sleep here on the stairs and then come along with you. You can't conceive how bored I've been, in that dashed play-box!'

For a moment Bernard hesitated.—It will be appreciated that in this most perilous prisoner-rescuing attempt he hadn't the backing of the M.P.A.S. The M.P.A.S. knew nothing about it, and he didn't mean to let even the Committee know he was going absent. ('The correspondence can just pile up!' thought Bernard.) He was operating entirely on his own, and *wanted* to operate on his own, just to show Miss Bianca he could rescue a prisoner on his own. Nevertheless the idea of having

Algernon for company wasn't disagreeable; and after a
moment's hesitation Bernard clasped the bear's paw with
grateful warmth.

Immediately, however, there was Nicodemus to be dis-
posed of.

'As my place here'll be shut up for probably several
days,' said Bernard firmly, 'I expect you'll be wanting to
be getting back home.'

'A hundred miles, on my crutches?' protested
Nicodemus reproachfully.

'Well, you got here,' pointed out Bernard.

'By means of a waggon bearing produce to the General
Store,' reminded Nicodemus, 'which will have long since
returned. Besides, I'm very comfortable where I am: I see
you've a very well stocked larder . . .'

So not only had he nosed into Bernard's sideboard, but
into his larder too!—From being merely firm Bernard
became absolutely adamant.

'No doubt there'll be some other waggon making the
trip tomorrow,' snapped he, 'which I strongly advise your
taking on its return journey. In fact, I insist on your taking
it, for mustn't you be there at Three Rivers to welcome
Miss Tomasina when I bring her back rescued?'

'But you must bring her back *here*,' protested
Nicodemus, 'out of the clutches of her wicked guardian
and to appear before the Board of Estates!'

Obviously he didn't mean to shift; and Bernard stamped
out onto the landing to blow off steam to Algernon.

'One thing I do know,' he exploded, 'I shall put my elderberry cordial under lock and key! *And* my larder! He can just starve!'

'The old are always selfish,' said Algernon philosophically. 'How well I wemember my own Gwandmother, after my Dad had been chewed to bits by a Corgi, first bursting into tears and then complaining there wasn't honey for tea!'

'There'll be honey for your breakfast,' promised Bernard. 'We'll have a good tuck in before we start, while let's hope Nicodemus is still asleep—and when he wakes up won't he get an unpleasant surprise!'

'And serve him wight,' agreed Algernon, 'for to make fwee with another chap's wine would get him blackballed from any decent club!—By the way,' he added thoughtfully, 'I suppose you've a plan for getting us *to* the Wolf Wange?'

'I'm just going to make one,' said Bernard, who actually hadn't yet given the matter serious thought. 'Our best bet of course would be by helicopter, only I don't know when the next one leaves.' (Miss Bianca would have known. Ever since her adventure in the Antarctic she always kept an affectionate eye on the helicopter schedules.) 'But trust the luck of the mice,' said Bernard, 'and let me look at a railway time-table.'

With which he stumped in again (and would have trod pretty heavily on Nicodemus's toes but that the latter, after so much elderberry cordial, was already nodding off), and after a short interval returned with whiskers a-cock.

'The very thing!' cried Bernard. 'There's a goods train

leaving at six a.m. bound for the foot-hills of the Wolf
Range bearing fodder for the mountain goats. We'll take
it in disguise.'

'As what?' asked Algernon.

'Why, as the fodder!' said resourceful Bernard. 'You're
stuffed with straw as it is, and where there's straw isn't
there always a mouse too? We'll have breakfast at five, and
then off to the station! It's going to be a piece of cheese!'

It was a measure of his excitement and resolution that
he'd quite forgotten about watering Miss Bianca's garden!

It wasn't altogether a piece of cheese, however. On arriving
at the station next morning after their good tuck in (which
for Algernon consisted of brown bread and butter and
honey and for Bernard of more cheese parings, bacon
rinds and piccalilli, eaten while Nicodemus still snored),
they were first almost drowned by a hose pipe washing
down the platform, then almost trampled to death by
porters not looking where they were going, then almost
squashed for good and all by one of the big fodder sacks
falling off a trolley. But this last misadventure actually
proved fortunate, for as it fell the sack split open at one
corner, and Bernard and Algernon were able to scramble
in among the hay and alfalfa; and unobserved by either
guard or driver were loaded onto the train on the first
stage of their perilous journey.

No bands played, as on the occasion of Bernard's and
Miss Bianca's foray to the salt mines. 'Twas just such an
anonymous departure as Bernard had hoped for!

To look ahead a bit, that the rat was let out of the bag was due to that old chatterbox Nicodemus. Some of Bernard's neighbours, calling to invite him to yet another wine-and-cheese party, found Nicodemus in residence instead; who to explain his presence immediately told them all about Bernard's heroic bid to rescue Miss Tomasina from bandits. But since the celebrated Miss Bianca wasn't involved, Bernard's frivolous neighbours weren't interested, and considered him merely foolhardy. However it made an amusing tale, and Bernard being unavailable for their wine-and-cheese parties, they invited Nicodemus instead —and didn't he punish the wine, besides taking home enough cheese to keep him going till next evening! Far from starving, he lived on the fat of the land, while the neighbours joked about Bernard's folly. They never thought of alerting the M.P.A.S.—as has been said, not one was even a member—still less of going to his aid themselves. Bernard was just as much on his own (except of course for Algernon) as he'd wanted to be.

To look ahead a bit again, never in the Wolf Range were they to see hair or hide of the Police!

6

IN THE WOLF RANGE

THE JOURNEY BY train was uneventful, but on their own indeed felt Bernard and Algernon when it finally halted at that last lonely station in the foot-hills of the Wolf Range, and the sacks were tossed out on the platform, and out from the damaged one they scrambled to survey the grim landscape . . .

All around stretched miles and miles of first rough heathery grass, then of snow, and there was a slight wind blowing—not a gentle breeze, but a creepy-crawly sort of wind that whined and whistled softly but persistently like the wind through the keyhole of a cupboard with a skeleton in it. No wonder the sacks were simply dumped, for the mountain goats to get at as best they could!

'I'll be glad to put into reverse,' said the engine-driver. 'I've always disliked these parts.'

'Me too,' said the guard. 'I've always felt there's something unnatural about them . . .'

'There's nothing unnatural about them at all,' said Bernard (bracingly) to Algernon, as the train puffed away. 'Everything in nature's naturally natural; the Wolf Range simply happens to be inhabited by ferocious wolves. Besides of course bandits in the higher-up fastnesses where they are holding Miss Tomasina captive, and whither we must now make our way.'

'You don't think they might be holding her captive somewhere a bit lower down?' suggested Algernon.

'As to that, naturally we shall enquire of local inhabitants as we proceed,' said Bernard, 'though in my opinion the higher (from a bandit's point of view) the better. Come on!'

It needed some courage and resolution on both their parts to leave the railway station—their last link with civilization!—and begin the long slog in search of the bandits' lair. All they knew was that they must go *up*—and up how many miles, when to gain but yards across rough grass was a toil, before they even reached the snow line? Bernard was nimble, and Algernon dogged, but whether they could have made it is doubtful—and in fact will never be known, since scarcely had they set out when both were bowled head over tip by a whole herd of mountain goats stampeding down to get at the fodder. Algernon, to use his own cricketing parlance, was hit for four, and Bernard would have been hit for a boundary but that he was fortunately (though unwittingly) fielded by the Billy-goat; and it says much for Bernard's presence of mind that even as he found himself clinging to a billy-goat's beard, as soon as he got his breath back he took the opportunity to make a first enquiry as to Miss Tomasina's whereabouts.

'There's something in my beard that *talks*!' snorted the

Billy-goat to his chief wife. (Like all billy-goats, he had several.) 'Get it out quick,' he snorted, rearing up in terror, 'it may be a goblin!'

Like all billy-goats, and indeed goats in general, he was highly superstitious. In olden days goats used to consort with witches, and as a race had never got over the effects of keeping such ill company. It may be said at once there were no goblins in the Wolf Range—just any fluttering broken bit of reed was a goblin to a goat.

'Pray do not be alarmed,' said Bernard hastily. 'I am no goblin but the Secretary of the M.P.A.S., here to rescue a young lady stolen by bandits; and if you'll only stand still a minute I'll get down by myself.'

With which he scrambled down by way of a long hairy foreleg, and as soon as he reached the ground took two steps back then one forward, and pulled his whiskers.

'At least he's got nice manners!' approved the she-goat. 'You are too impetuous, my love!'

'It's me who was too impetuous,' apologized Bernard, 'in seeking news of Miss Tomasina before I'd properly introduced myself. Now that I *have*, you may be of valuable assistance.'

'No one who comes impersonating a goblin can expect any assistance from *me*,' snorted the Billy-goat, still angrily—for he'd begun to think he'd made a bit of a fool of himself.

'But I didn't,' persisted Bernard. 'At least not by intention.'

'Fur and a long tail!' accused the Billy-goat.

'I'm afraid I can't do without either,' said Bernard, 'but at least I haven't seven-toed feet, which I believe is also the mark of goblins. If you'll just let me re-cap—'

'Do, my love!' begged the she-goat of her husband.

'—I am here to rescue a missing young lady believed stolen by bandits into the upper fastnesses of these mountains; and you being obviously more familiar with those upper fastnesses than anyone else, perhaps you've seen her?'

'Nary hair nor hide!' declared the Billy-goat.

'But I think *I* may have,' said his wife. 'Didn't I tell you, my love, of the young thing straying out of the bandits' encampment who stroked my coat and called me Nanny?'

'You said it was a boy,' reminded her husband.

'So I did,' agreed the she-goat. 'Perhaps it's *two* poor young things the bandits have captured!'

'All the fodder will be eaten up already,' snorted the Billy-goat, 'if we don't make a move!'—and so saying swept her down with all the rest of his harem towards the sacks still lying on the railway platform. If horns and hooves had clashed before, even more did they clash now!

'Where are you, Algernon?' called Bernard, looking anxiously about for his friend. 'Where are you, are you all right?'

'As well as one could expect,' replied the bear, painfully picking himself up from a clump of heather, 'after being hit for a four. I didn't land as soft as you, old chap: *I* landed on someone's hoof, and shall pwobably bear the scar on my tum for the west of my life.'

'It'll be an honourable one,' said Bernard, 'and at least we've learned from these harum-scarum animals that Miss Tomasina is indeed somewhere in the upper fastnesses—for that the bandits have disguised her as a boy is more than likely! And I've an idea,' he added. 'After plundering the sacks, won't they be making *back* into those upper fastnesses, and why shouldn't we hitch a lift? Hang on to a tail, as I will too, and we'll be beyond the snow line before you can say tin-opener. Are you game?'

'If we both stick together!' said Algernon.

So as soon as the herd started careering back both jumped at the tail of a nanny-goat obviously expecting twins (and thus wouldn't notice the extra weight), and up both were carried without further effort on their part to well above the snow line. It was a piece of cheese indeed!

They were actually well above the snow line when the Billy-goat's chief wife, who had been keeping a benevolent eye on the expectant mother of twins, suggested the latter's taking a rest. 'You must look after yourself!' said she kindly. 'If you want to rest a moment, I'll wait with you . . .'

But the expectant mother of twins wouldn't, she was too conceited, and just to show how perfectly fit and well she was, flirted up her tail in such a flourish, Bernard and Algernon were flung off it and on she cantered!

'Never mind,' said Bernard, as they picked themselves up. 'Just think what miles and miles we've covered! I dare say the bandits' lair is but a couple of steps away!'

Unfortunately, scarcely had they taken the first step when the snow gave way beneath them and they found themselves not in the lair of bandits but in that of a wolf; and though neither parent wolf was at home, what sharp teeth and drooling lips had their four cubs!

7

THE WOLF CUBS

THEIR NAMES WERE Red, Rufus, Russet and Ruby (their little sister), and they were waiting for their mother to come back from hunting with their tongues hanging out. As Bernard and Algernon tumbled in between their paws, they squealed with pleasure just like the young ladies in the Boarding School—but obviously with no idea of making pets of them!

'Here's at least something to keep us going till Ma gets back!' cried Red, 'I don't know what sort of meat the bigger one is, but for my part I'm hungry enough to eat a mouse!'

'It looks quite a *plump* mouse,' said Rufus. 'We'll eat *it* first!'

(How often Bernard had meant to get his weight down, and now how he wished he *had*!)

'It won't go far amongst the four of us,' objected Russet. 'I know what! We'll do eeny-meeny-miny-mo, and the one who gets "he" shall have it!'

'You can count *me* out straightaway,' put in the kinder-hearted Ruby.

'All the better,' said Rufus. 'That leaves only three of us.

—Red, you're the biggest; you start.'

'Eeny-meeny-miny-mo—' began Red.

'Catch a rabbit by the toe—' chimed in Rufus.

'If it hollers, let it go!' chimed in Russet. 'One, two, three—'

'And out goes he! It's me!' cried Red, pouncing.

Only just before he pounced, Ruby shot out a paw and scooped Bernard into her own mouth!

'Unfair, unfair!' cried all her brothers. 'Just *like* a girl!' they cried. 'Put him back into circulation at once!'

But Ruby merely showed her teeth.—She didn't dare do more for fear of actually swallowing Bernard, which was far from her intent. (Though he, finding himself in a dark red cavern barred with ivory, couldn't know.) Meanwhile Algernon, with absolutely heroic self-sacrifice, had thrust his head down between his arms, and drawn up his legs, and was trying to look like a trussed fowl. Actually the wolf cubs had never seen a fowl properly trussed; the snow geese their mother occasionally brought home were all dangling necks and feet; but pretending to be a trussed fowl Algernon looked so much plumper than usual, Red and Rusty and Rufus were ready to have a go at him, and indeed he would have come to a sudden end had not the she-wolf at that moment come home.

She came home in a very bad temper. She had hunted all night long, but unsuccessfully; and besides being very hungry herself, knew her cubs would be bothering her for milk, which she really hadn't got to give them. So she immediately boxed their ears all round, and cuffed their

noses for good measure, and declared that she was so worn
out she was going straight to sleep and if one of them let
out so much as a whimper he'd wish he'd never been born
a wolf cub.

'But look, Ma, what we've got!' cried Rufus.

'A bag of straw?' said the she-wolf, sniffing Algernon
contemptuously. 'You should know better than to try and
eat *straw*!'

'Well, Ruby's got a mouse in her mouth,' declared
Red.

'I never thought to see a daughter of mine descend to
vermin,' said the she-wolf. 'Is this true, Ruby?'

Ruby had just time to cough Bernard up before answering no.

'I'm glad to hear it,' said the she-wolf, flipping both Bernard and Algernon out of the lair with one flick of her great paw, 'but I'm sure no more troublesome litter of cubs has ever been born!'

Nonetheless, as she curled up in the innermost recesses of the lair, she let Red and Rufus and Rusty and Ruby snuggle in beside her under her brush.

But in what piteous state were Algernon and Bernard— the bear quite muscle-bound from pretending to be a trussed fowl, and Bernard dripping saliva from Ruby's jaws! Despite their more than uncomfortable situation the latter's first impulse was to get himself clean—mice so hate anything sticky or slimy on their coats.

'Get out of that ridiculous lotus-position and help rub me down with snow!' he adjured Algernon. 'Is this a time to be practising Zen?'

'Actually I was impersonating a twussed fowl,' said Algernon reproachfully, 'in the hope of diverting the wolf cubs' attention . . .'

'Forgive me,' said Bernard. 'What heroism, what self-sacrifice, what *imagination*! Can *I* help you get your legs into their usual hanging-down position?'

'Well, a little massage would help,' said Algernon.

So Bernard massaged Algernon's lower limbs until he was able to stand upright again, and then Algernon shampooed Bernard with snow until his fur was quite clean again, and both felt much better, and Bernard realized that in considering Algernon no more that a soft toy he'd quite misjudged the bear.

'Never,' said Bernard solemnly, 'have I met with a stouter hearted fellow adventurer. Not even Nils, with whom I adventured to the Black Castle, was stouter hearted! Your name shall be inscribed in the M.P.A.S. Records Book as soon as we get back.'

'Thanks aw'fly,' said Algernon. 'As you know, I'd like a little lustre added to it. *Now* where do we go? Not up again, I hope?'

'Certainly not,' said Bernard. 'We're so far above the snow line already, I dare say the bandits' lair is so close, only a slight further effort, on the level, will enable us to reach it.'

'Couldn't we take a bit of an easy first?' suggested Algernon. (Although as stout hearted as Nils, he wasn't quite so active.) 'After all that jolting about on goats, and then those wolf cubs, I know *I'm* weady for one!'

So, as a matter of fact, was Bernard.

'If there was any shelter to be had I'd agree with you,' said he. 'Only there isn't.'

'Well, what's that over there?' said Algernon.

Bernard looked where the bear was pointing, and saw an old Wellington boot sticking out of the snow like a small, dilapidated, toppling lighthouse.—Whose its owner had been, and where the other was, they never discovered; but in fact it was all that was left to tell the tale of a mountaineer who should have known better than to go climbing in Wellies anyway. Now its black rubbery walls afforded a welcome shelter, and within them Algernon and Bernard soon sank into exhausted slumber. They were so tired they slept the clock round and then the clock round again—Algernon dreaming of happy days in London, and Bernard (more gratefully) of the Duke of Wellington.

'*Who is this valorous and intrepid mouse I see before me?*' said the Duke of Wellington, in Bernard's dream. '*Is it he who routed the French cavalry at Waterloo?*'

(Miss Bianca always did history with the Boy, so Bernard had naturally picked up a bit too.)

'*Indeed he is,*' said the Duke of Wellington's aide-de-camp, '*by nipping behind all their horses' tails!*'

(This was a memory from Bernard's experiences in the Orient, when he'd played polo for the Princely Orchids.)

'*Then introduce him to Queen Victoria at once,*' said the Duke of Wellington, '*to be knighted for gallantry on the field!*'

'*Arise, Sir Bernard,*' pronounced Queen Victoria, and immediately turned into a Camembert cheese . . .

It was only a dream, and even in his sleep Bernard suspected it was only a dream, but it was a very agreeable one. He'd have been happy to dream on and on, in the Wellington boot; but when a second dawn dawned he woke up and remembered Miss Tomasina.

'Out we go!' he adjured Algernon, 'on the last lap!'

'I'd just dweamed I'd been taken to tea at the Savoy Hotel,' yawned Algernon. 'What cakes, what ices! But out we'll go if you say so; I feel quite a new bear!'

So off they set in good spirits towards the (they hoped) now quite close bandits' lair where Miss Tomasina (they hoped) was being held captive.

8

BACK AT THE EMBASSY

WHY THE AMBASSADRESS and her son returned from the mountain resort a week earlier than they'd intended was partly because the Boy seemed completely recovered, and partly because the Ambassador's letters were getting dolefuller and dolefuller. ('*My dearest love,*' he wrote, '*I can't tell you how I miss you, and where are my thick pyjamas?*') Also there had been several thefts from the hotels round about, of fur coats—there were also thefts from the hotels' store-rooms, but these the hoteliers could and did keep quiet about—and the Ambassadress certainly didn't want to lose her sables! So as the Boy seemed quite himself again, she decided to return—to the extreme joy of Miss Bianca, who while the Ambassadress packed composed a brief but heartfelt quatrain.

BRIEF BUT HEARTFELT QUATRAIN
COMPOSED BY MISS BIANCA WHILE
THE AMBASSADRESS WAS LOOKING
FOR THE BOY'S ANORAK
'*Farewell the lake, farewell the snows,*
Farewell each sparkling Christmas tree!

How far, far dearer is to me
The humblest flower that in my garden grows!'
                                    M.B.

But what a sight met her eyes as that evening she re-entered
it! All was dry as a bone. The little pink daisy had died
absolutely; even the hardiest of her flowers, such as
nasturtiums, were drooping on their stalks. Miss Bianca
couldn't believe her eyes—she'd so trusted in Bernard to

look after them! Immediately, she jumped on the spring of the Venetian glass fountain—but it will be remembered that Bernard had turned it off. 'What *can* have happened?' wondered Miss Bianca. Then the thought occurred to her that perhaps Bernard too had been smitten by mumps!— and without even setting foot over her porcelain threshold, off she hurried to his flat in the cigar-cabinet, prepared to nurse him if necessary day and night.

She knocked and rang at the door. There was no answer. 'Is he unable to get out of bed even?' Miss Bianca asked herself. (Actually it was Nicodemus who wasn't able to get out of bed between one wine-and-cheese party and the next.) She knocked and knocked, until several of Bernard's neighbours came out of their front doors to see what was going on.

'Why, Miss Bianca, how delightful to have you back!' cried Bernard's neighbours. 'The Boy is perfectly recovered, we hope? Did you have a pleasant time at the resort?'

'Yes, no,' replied Miss Bianca briefly. 'Pray give me news of Bernard! Is he ill?'

'Ill? Good gracious, no!' cried all Bernard's neighbours. 'Don't you know, Miss Bianca—but of course you wouldn't, you've been away—he's gone off on some prisoner-rescuing wild goose chase into the Wolf Range!'

And they repeated all Nicodemus had told them about Bernard's bid to rescue Miss Tomasina from bandits, just as an amusing tale. But not in the least amused was Miss Bianca; her whiskers quivered with apprehension!

'You mean Bernard is in the Wolf Range *alone*?' she exclaimed.

'I believe there's a teddy bear with him,' said the optician—actually he who'd persuaded Bernard to buy his long-distance glasses. 'Won't you join me in a glass of sherry, Miss Bianca?'

'In the Wolf Range, among bandits, accompanied by no more than a soft toy!' exclaimed Miss Bianca.

'According to Nicodemus,' said the chartered accountant. 'Actually my wife and I were just going to shake up a cocktail . . .'

'What *I* believe Miss Bianca would like best is a *tisane*,' said the doctor, 'such as *my* wife is brewing this very moment from lime-blossoms . . .'

For everyone wanted to enjoy the prestige of a visit from the celebrated Miss Bianca!

'How very kind of all of you, but thank you, no,' said she. 'After so long an absence I have my garden to attend to!—You mentioned a Nicodemus,' she added. 'Where is *he* to be found?'

'Why, just over the way in Bernard's flat,' said the optician, 'where Bernard left him in charge. And no wonder your knocking didn't wake him, Miss Bianca— between one wine-and-cheese party and the next he's dead to the world!'

'Thank you again,' said Miss Bianca, with a graceful bow that so obviously preluded her departure, all Bernard's neighbours withdrew into their own flats. But as soon as they *were* withdrawn, once more she rat-tatted on Bernard's door.

By this time Nicodemus was stirring and opened up; and instantly by her ermine fur and the silver chain about her neck he recognized Miss Bianca.

'Miss Bianca!' he cried. ''Tis you at last! Oh that you had returned earlier, for 'tis you alone, I always knew, could rescue my dear young lady!'

With which he repeated in more detail the tale Miss Bianca had already heard from Bernard's neighbours—though omitting his own bloomer in having first despatched Bernard into a boarding school for young ladies; when Miss Bianca asked how Bernard came to be accompanied by a teddy bear, Nicodemus said merely that the bear happened to be taking the same train.

'And how long have they been gone?' asked Miss Bianca anxiously.

'Four or five days,' said Nicodemus. 'Time is running out, for Miss Tomasina's birthday, when as I told you she must claim her inheritance, is on the twentieth of this month—so barely a week remains for her to be rescued in! But if only *you* will go after them,' begged Nicodemus, 'then their efforts may be crowned with success indeed!'

It was now Miss Bianca showed her true greatness of spirit. She *could* have gone after them, by a helicopter she knew bound for a survey of the Wolf Range the very next day. (Ever since being rescued by one from the Antarctic, she always kept an affectionate eye on the helicopter schedules!) But with a leap of imagination she realized that Bernard had gone off on his own because he

wanted to go off on his own!

'*I* think we may safely leave the whole operation to Bernard,' said she, 'while I for my part see to my garden!'

Nonetheless so distressed was Miss Bianca to think of Bernard penetrating the Wolf Range with no stouter companion than a soft toy—she hadn't yet met Algernon, so knew nothing of his straw-filled fibre—she wasn't her usual self at all.

In the Embassy schoolroom life resumed its even tenor; just as usual each morning found Miss Bianca seated on the

Boy's shoulder to help him with his arithmetic or geography. But she was so absent-minded, it was often the Boy, not she, who found out an error in addition, or that he'd mistakenly placed the Alps in India instead of Switzerland. In a way it was a good thing, because it meant he had to think for himself more instead of relying on Miss Bianca; but 'twas a very novel sensation for her not to be the corrector herself!

'I hope *you're* not sickening for mumps?' said the Boy anxiously. 'I couldn't bear it if it was me you caught them off!'

Miss Bianca exerted herself to frisk about in a decidedly un-mumpish way. But the Boy knew her too well to be taken in.

'Then something's worrying you,' said he, 'and I believe I know what it is: you're upset about your garden! I noticed myself it looked all dried up. If the fountain isn't working, I'll soon put *that* right!'

So he did, by merely turning the tap on again; and with jars and jars of water Miss Bianca revived at least her nasturtiums. The little pink daisy, alas, was too far gone . . .

POEM WRITTEN BY MISS BIANCA
AFTER WATERING HER NASTURTIUMS
      'Crimson and yellow,
        Amber and gold,
          Striped like a tiger
           On the banks of the Niger,
    Was ever a flower
        So hardy and bold?

> *Without you my garden*
> *Would lose half its charm*
> *But oh my dear Bernard,*
>   *I do hope you won't come to harm!'*
>   M.B.

It will be seen that the last two lines of this poem had
nothing to do with the eight preceding. Miss Bianca
recognized the unmatchingness herself, but hadn't been able
not to bring Bernard in, she was so worried about him!

The Ambassadress back, and with Christmas approaching, the Embassy was gayer than ever. Folk dancers
danced in the forecourt, string quartets played Mozart
in the music-room, in the banquet hall there was a
banquet and in the ballroom a ball. The Boy took part in
all these festivities with even more than usual enjoyment,
but Miss Bianca, instead of attending them all from his
pocket—on one occasion hadn't she tripped forth to make
her bow to the French Ambassador?—regularly pleaded
a headache.

'Poor Miss Bianca! I'm afraid the mountain air didn't
do as much for you as it did for my son,' said the
Ambassadress kindly. 'No doubt the altitude was too much
for you?'

With a graceful droop of her right-hand whiskers Miss
Bianca indicated that the altitude had indeed been too
much for her, then with an upward flirt of her left-hand
set indicated that she'd soon be all right again, so that the
Ambassadress wasn't to worry. Miss Bianca's were the
most accomplished whiskers imaginable!

'Then you must just stay quiet and snug in your Porcelain Pagoda,' said the Ambassadress kindly.

Snug and quiet indeed could have been Miss Bianca, but for her ever increasing anxiety about Bernard . . .

'Oh Bernard,' cried Miss Bianca mentally, 'if only I knew where you *were*!'

It was just as well she didn't know, because—

9

THE AVALANCHE

—BERNARD AND ALGERNON with him were now buried beneath an avalanche.

It had struck, as avalanches usually do, with no more warning than a slight pause in the creepy-crawly wind, only minutes after the pair emerged from the Wellington boot. One moment all was still; the next, with sudden ferocious speed, a great wave of snow crashed down like a demented elephant (only many times larger), and only the fortunate proximity of a clump of eidelweiss saved them from immediate extinction. Eidelweiss can stand up to anything—it has to—but even the eidelweiss crouched almost flat before such an onslaught, and even flatter crouched Bernard and Algernon under its roots.— Instinctively they burrowed further, into a hollow beyond; and there huddled trembling and for the moment speechless.

'That's torn it!' gasped Bernard at last. 'There's no getting out through *that* blockade! Even in the Antarctic I don't remember such a dreadful occurrence!—Oh, my dear friend,' he added remorsefully, 'to what an icy grave have I led you, for no doubt our corpses will be found, if

they ever are, frozen stiff as boards!'

'Yours may be,' said Algernon, 'but stuffed with straw as I am, I'll be found almost as good as new. But I'll always remember you, old chap; is there anywhere particular you'd like to be buried?'

'Yes,' said Bernard. 'In some nice warm, rich, steamy manure.'

Where he'd really have liked to be buried was in the Pagoda garden, only he felt it would be too distressing for Miss Bianca to see his tomb every time she watered her flowers. So he said in manure—the thought of which, in his present semi-frozen state, indeed appealed to him almost as much.

'I'll do my best,' promised Algernon, 'but we're not dead *yet*!'

Bernard pulled himself together.

'You're right,' he agreed, more cheerfully, 'which considering our experiences with those wolf cubs is a bit of a miracle in itself. We're not dead yet!'

'Excelsior!' murmured the eidelweiss approvingly.

'I beg your pardon?' said Bernard.

'I was quoting a poem,' explained the eidelweiss. '"A youth, who bore, 'mid snow and ice, A banner with the strange device, Excelsior!"'

'Poor chap,' said Bernard feelingly.

'Actually it means "Keep going",' said the eidelweiss. 'And since you seem in some difficulty as to getting out the *front* way, why not try the *back*?'

'But is there one?' asked Algernon.

'Certainly,' said the eidelweiss. 'Where you are used to be the entrance to a fox's runway, so naturally there's a back door too. Now I really can't talk any more—I'm half choked by snow as it is!'

'Wolves are bad enough, but foxes even worse,' said Bernard. 'Foxes will eat anything, even vermin.' (Being called vermin still rankled.) 'However, since it seems our only chance, I suppose we'd better have a shot at the back way—though if we do meet a fox it'll be all up with me at least!'

Algernon this time in the lead, they cautiously explored the back part of the hollow, from which a quite sizeable tunnel indeed opened out; they entered it and nosed cautiously on. Overhead the avalanche still crashed with a noise like that of gunfire; but after a little they could hear it no more, and all was still . . .

The stillness became quite uncanny. Instinctively, they spoke in whispers . . .

Once or twice they had to skirt the skull of a snow-rabbit, or its hind-leg bones—proof indeed that foxes had used that runway! ('I don't see any skeletons of mice,' whispered Algernon encouragingly. 'No; *they're* crunched up, bones and all,' whispered back Bernard.) However no fox did they encounter, and for a very good reason which will shortly be disclosed.

And at least, from the gradient of the ground, they were still going up—that is, towards the bandits' lair, not down and so away from it. This had both an advantage and a *dis*; it gave them hope, but made the going all the more toil-some. ('First those stairs in the Young Ladies' Boarding School—!' though Bernard. 'Of all the uphill adventures—!') He was glad indeed not to have Miss Bianca with him; her delicate limbs could never have supported the fatigue. But on Bernard and Algernon plodded.—A plod was rather Algernon's natural gait, except when escaping from an incinerator, but Bernard, like all mice, was used to proceed by short runs, and the enforced slowness of the pace made it all the more wearisome. Also it was now days since either had had anything to eat, and they were absolutely famished.

'Honey,' said Algernon suddenly. 'That's what I'd like to get down to—a great big jar of honey. What would *you* like to get down to?'

'Bacon rinds,' said Bernard unhesitatingly. 'Though I don't say a bit of cheese would come amiss.'

'Nor a slice of brown bread–and–butter,' said Algernon, 'just to give the honey body . . .'

'Sardine-tails . . .,' mused Bernard.

'Cold rice pudding with condensed milk on it . . .,' mused Algernon.

It is common knowledge that the minds of all explorers tend to dwell on food, so Bernard and Algernon weren't particularly greedy exceptions; but what *was* exceptional was that scarcely had each finished describing what he liked best when the tunnel suddenly opened out into a large low cave absolutely crammed with their favourite foods!

Besides the bottles of wine ranged round its rocky walls, were sides of bacon, sweet-cured hams, tins of sardines and condensed milk, jars of honey and pots of jam—many of the latter leaking their rich contents into one glorious, many-coloured, many-flavoured mess. As the Persian poet once remarked (though in rather different circum-stances), if there was Paradise on earth, it was here!

So at least felt Bernard and Algernon. For fully half-an-hour they just munched and munched—Algernon switch-ing from honey to jam to condensed milk, while Bernard stuck to bacon. For fully half-an-hour neither uttered a word—their mouths were too full. Then—

'What a perfectly magnificent larder!' admired Algernon. 'Whoever do you suppose could have stocked it?'

'Explorers, of course,' said Bernard. 'I remember seeing just such a cache myself, in the Antarctic. But I must say whoever *these* explorers were, they did themselves jolly well!'

Algernon, his appetite temporarily sated, began to look about a bit.

'Did *your* explorers have hurdy-gurdies with them?' he asked.

'Not that I remember,' said Bernard. 'Why?'

'There's a couple over in that corner,' said Algernon. 'You're making a mistake, old man, not to try this condensed milk!'

'First things first,' said Bernard, 'and the first thing with me is always bacon.'

Even on a whole side of bacon Bernard had by now left an impression, for as soon as his first hunger was assuaged he'd nibbled out the initials M.B. on its rind; and was just beginning to nibble a heart round them when Algernon spoke again.

'Well, did they have fur coats with them?'

'Of course,' said Bernard. 'No one could go exploring the Antarctic without a fur coat. What's on your mind?'

'All *those* fur coats,' said Algernon, nodding towards a rack of coat-hangers that almost filled one wall, 'look to me as though they'd belonged to ladies. I'm sure one's a mink, and another a sable . . .'

Now that Bernard took a look too he saw that the fur

coats hanging up on the hangers weren't in the least like any an explorer would wear—they were far too fancy!

'D'you know what *I* think?' said Algernon. 'I don't believe we're in any explorers' cache at all . . . *I* believe it's the bandits' store-room we're in!'

Which in fact was the case—and glad would the hoteliers at the mountain resort have been to know where their lady visitors' fur coats had disappeared to—let alone all the

stores from their store-rooms! Algernon's guess was right:
the bandits had moved in (which was why the foxes had
moved out), and adapted the cave at the back door of the
runway to their own nefarious purposes. They'd shored
up the roof, and put shelving round the walls, and slung
up racks to hang the stolen fur coats on, and in short made
it as complete a robbers' store house as could be imagined.
They didn't bother to do anything about the front
entrance—none of the bandits could have got through it
anyway—but entered and exited by way of a cleft under
an overhanging rock which Bernard and Algernon hadn't
yet discovered.

'By gum!' said Bernard, gazing round in turn. 'I
believe you're right!'

'Then we can't be all that far from their lair,' said
Algernon.

'Right again!' agreed Bernard. 'I dare say it's quite
close . . . Do you hear anything?'

'Like what?' asked Algernon.

'It sounded to *me*,' said Bernard, 'like banditish voices
uplifted in song.'

Both listened intently.

'"O sole mio"?' suggested Algernon.

'Something like that,' said Bernard, 'with a bit of
"Funiculi-funicula' thrown in . . .'

In fact it was the sound of song that guided them to the
cleft under the overhanging rock. They peered cautiously
forth; outside it was now night, but the darkness was
partially dispersed by the flames of an enormous bonfire,
as well as by the glow from a lesser one serving a culinary

purpose. For the bandits were holding a barbecue. A stolen goat roasted on a spit, wine circulated like water, as with voices uplifted in 'O sole mio', 'Funiculi-funicula', and other popular airs, the bandits celebrated another year's successful robbing.

10

THE BANDITS' BARBECUE

HOW VILLAINOUS WERE THE faces revealed by the firelight! All were heavily mustachioed, some bearded; some were scarred from old knife wounds, others pock-marked by gunpowder; but the teeth of all gleamed white and sharp as the wolf cubs'! The Chief Bandit (for so he obviously was, by the way he ordered all the rest about) was the most villainous looking of all; in addition to mustachios and beard he wore a patch over one eye, so that almost nothing could be seen of his face *except* his teeth; and what made his appearance even more dreadful, the patch wasn't even a plain black one, but white, with a black cross painted on it. Thus when he was referred to as Cross-eye, it didn't mean he squinted—indeed the glance from his other eye was as bold and piercing as an eagle's!

But at least he had the grace to say grace. As the goat began to be carved up—

'Silence, all!' he commanded. (All the bandits stopped singing and bowed their heads.) 'For what we have received, may we be truly thankful!'

'To our heroic leader,' murmured all the bandits.

'*Now* if you care to burst into song again—'

'For he's a jolly good fellow,' carolled all the bandits,
'For he's a jolly good fellow,
For he's a jolly good fellow,
And so say all of us!'

'Very nice,' approved Cross-eye. 'Now before you all
start making pigs of yourselves, I ask you to raise your
glasses in a toast to our friend with the hurdy-gurdy, who
so cleverly discovered which were the best hotels to rob,
and to whom in fact we owe this excellent claret.'

'Twas no true travelling showman but a bandit who'd
played the hurdy-gurdy in the sideshow at the circus at the
mountain resort! (The Boy had actually set his eyes on
him—and *whom else had he set eyes on*?) As the hurdy-gurdy
player rose to his feet and bowed, and all the rest cried
'Hear, hear'—

'Not forgetting his nephew—or should it be niece?'
added someone slyly.

The Chief Bandit looked benign, or rather as benign as
he could, with one eye concealed by a patch with a cross
on it.

'Not forgetting, as you say, his assistant—who after
the dull life he or she led with his or her guardian I dare
say wouldn't now exchange his or her lot for any number
of estates!—Why isn't she or he taking part in our
celebrations?'

'He or she said she was too tired,' explained the hurdy-
gurdy player. 'Ever since both my waltzing mice dropped
down dead, he or she's been complaining of head-
aches . . .'

'Then a little gaiety will do him or her nothing but

good,' decided Cross-eye. 'Go and fetch him or her at
once!'

Off the hurdy-gurdy player obediently hastened; and
Bernard and Algernon, who had of course been listening
with all their ears, fairly trembled with excitement at the
prospect of at last beholding the missing heiress!

For now they were quite sure Bernard's guess had been
right, and the bandits *had* disguised Miss Tomasina as a boy,
in order to throw pursuers off the track!

'Now is the time to display all our resource and
heroism,' breathed Bernard, 'to rescue her from under the
bandits' very mustachios! Be prepared to do or die!'

'Or if she *is* happier as she is,' breathed back Algernon,
'couldn't we just pack the whole thing in?'

'You know little of the principles of the M.P.A.S.,'
breathed Bernard. 'A prisoner's to be rescued, like it or
not!'

The point however remained academic, for when the
hurdy-gurdy player returned dragging Miss Tomasina by
the wrist, it was all too apparent that far from being
happy she was in the last stages of wretchedness . . .

Pitiable indeed was the small, slight figure now introduced upon the festive scene. Her hair cut short, in rough
goatskin breeches and goatskin cap, so like a starveling
boy she looked, Bernard couldn't have been certain she
was Miss Tomasina at all, save that as she advanced into the
firelight there showed up on her right cheek the very mole
Nicodemus had described!

Poor, pitiable Miss Tomasina! The bunch of ribbons in her cap seemed to mock the sadness of the pale, pinched face beneath, with a deep wrinkle between the brows and lips that uncontrollably trembled. She looked about at the bonfires as though she scarcely saw them; she had eyes only for the Chief Bandit; and instinctively dropped a curtsey . . .

'Forgetting yourself again!' chided the hurdy-gurdy player.

Whereupon Miss Tomasina awkwardly bowed instead and made as though to pull her forelock.—How many tenants or peasants had pulled their forelocks to *her*, as she rode about her estates! Now it was she who pulled hers to the Chief Bandit!

'I'm sorry,' she apologized, in a small, weak voice. 'I didn't know my presence was required . . .'

'Certainly it's required,' said the Chief Bandit, still with a benign look. 'Now that you are one of us, rejoicings, as well as perils, should be shared!'

'Only I've such a headache,' murmured Miss Tomasina.

The Chief Bandit now fixed her with his other eye—or rather with the patch with the cross on it—and Miss Tomasina stared at it as though hypnotized.

'Of course if you tell me to I must,' she murmured, 'stay and join in your rejoicings . . .'

'You say that willingly and of your own accord?' demanded the Chief Bandit.

'Willingly and of my own accord . . .,' repeated Miss Tomasina.

'And you haven't a headache after all?'

'No, I haven't a headache after all . . .'

'And there's nothing you'd like better than to join in our merriment?'

'Nothing I'd like better . . .,' echoed Miss Tomasina.

'Well, *we* want no such death's head at our feast,' suddenly snarled the Chief Bandit. 'I had meant to reward you with a sable coat—'

'But I *have* a sable coat!' interrupted Miss Tomasina. 'At least,' she added bewilderedly, 'I used to have one . . .'

'Take her away before she remembers too much!' ordered the Chief Bandit, 'and give her more of that poppy tea!—Now let each eat his fill!'

All the rest were only too glad to do so, while the hurdy-gurdy player hastily conducted his assistant away from the festive scene; and as they skirted the bonfires and disappeared into the shadows, so did Bernard and Algernon.

It needed some heroism on their part indeed to leave their hiding place in the cleft under the rock; but cleverly they avoided the patches of light thrown by the bonfires, stuck to the shadows, and were almost on the hurdy-gurdy player's heels as he and Miss Tomasina reached a small waterproof shelter (made from stolen mackintoshes), whence the hurdy-gurdy player, instead of brewing more poppy tea for his charge, immediately hurried back to join in the celebrations—which naturally he didn't want to miss, he himself cutting so prominent a figure in them!

As soon as he was out of hearing—

'Miss Tomasina!' whispered Bernard, through a flap in the waterproof tent.

There was no answer. Bernard and Algernon crept in, and beheld Miss Tomasina lying face down on a rough straw pallet, shaken by deep drawn sobs that racked her whole slender frame.—Many of her tenants had to seek repose on just such pallets, but it is to be hoped none had ever cause to weep so!

'Miss Tomasina!' repeated Bernard, more urgently; and now she looked up.

'Who is it that calls me by my rightful name?' she marvelled.

'Me, Bernard,' replied Bernard, 'come with my friend Algernon to rescue you from being kidnapped!'

'What!' exclaimed the missing heiress. 'Have the Police been sent to look for me at last?—But no,' she added disappointedly, 'you're only a mouse and a teddy bear!'

Bernard, if not Algernon, was used to this reaction on the part of prisoners.

'I also happen to be,' he pointed out, 'the Secretary of the M.P.A.S., or Mouse Prisoners' Aid Society, while one of Algernon's ancestors was named after a President of the great American Republic. You may place every confidence in us.'

He spoke more bravely than he felt, for at that moment he had no idea how they actually *would* effect Miss Tomasina's rescue. He just trusted in the luck of the mice.

'I beg your pardon,' said Miss Tomasina. 'Who but I should appreciate the heroism of mice? It was the Waltzing Mice who saved me from complete obliviousness by drinking up half the poppy tea the bandits gave me, and so sank into oblivion themselves!'

'How did you get kidnapped in the first place?' asked Algernon curiously.

'I hardly remember,' said Miss Tomasina. 'I was walking in my own woods when an old man with a hurdy-gurdy came up and wanted to show me how prettily his mice danced. So I went with him to where their cage was—no farther than the next clearing!—and then when I'd seen them he offered me a cup of tea, which I felt I couldn't refuse, he was so humble and pressing. Little did I know it was poppy tea, that steals away all will and memory! For the next thing I knew,' said Miss Tomasina, 'I was far, far from home—and somehow hypnotized by a cross . . .'

'If you mean on the Chief Bandit's eye-patch,' said Algernon, 'it's only like the one in noughts-and-crosses.'

But Miss Tomasina shuddered.

'You can't have really looked at it,' shuddered she. 'It grows first larger, then smaller, then shrinks into a little ink spot, then grows larger again . . . Whatever he told me to do I knew I'd have to—even to going out disguised as a boy with the hurdy-gurdy player and his Waltzing Mice! I only hope I made their last moments happy,' sighed Miss Tomasina, 'by playing their favourite tunes!'

'Everything you tell us promotes our sympathy for you,' said Bernard. 'Are you quite yourself again now?'

'Indeed I am,' said Miss Tomasina, 'and place myself entirely in your hands!'

This was a bit of a facer for Bernard, who as has been

said had as yet no solid plan for rescuing her; but just at that moment—trust the luck of the mice!—he heard overhead the chipper-chopper flipper-flapper of a helicopter about to land!

II

UP AND AWAY!

IT CAME AS A complete surprise to him, since unlike Miss
Bianca he'd never kept an eye on the helicopter schedules;
but he recognized the sound from his experience in the
Antarctic, and at once took heart. As indeed he was right
to, for the helicopter Pilot, mistaking the bonfires for a
flare-path, landed his machine within a hundred yards of
the bandits' barbecue!

In what disarray all the bandits scattered! They were
courageous enough to rob hotels, or waylay solitary
travellers, but not to face anything out of their narrow
though nefarious experience. Moreover anyone in uni-
form was anathema to them, and as the Pilot with gold
braid on his sleeve leaned out, each and all fled—some
clutching a last fragment of goat's meat, others a half
empty glass—back and down through the cleft into the
safety of their cavern. Even Cross-eye fled!

'Extraordinary,' said the Pilot, leaning out. 'These
certainly aren't regulation flares!'

'They look to me more like bonfires,' said his Navigator,
leaning out in turn, 'probably lit by some of those silly
idiots at the hotels . . .'

'We'll just have to take off again,' said the Pilot.

'Not without us!' yelled Bernard.

Bernard dashed so impetuously from the mackintosh tent his whiskers were singed by the bonfires' sparks. So was Algernon's fur singed, as he followed after yelling, 'Help, help, HELP!'

'Curious effect these mountain winds have,' said the Pilot. 'I had the illusion of someone shouting help . . . Well, off we go again!'

But by this time Miss Tomasina had stumbled out after her saviours, and the sound of her desperate voice pierced even above the noise of the helicopter about to take off.

'Stop! Wait!' she cried. 'Wait for *me*, Miss Tomasina!'

'Good heavens!' exclaimed the Pilot. 'The missing heiress all have been seeking high and low! What extraordinary luck has enabled us to find you here?'

Bernard could have told him it was the luck of the mice, but hadn't a chance to.

'Take us on board at once!' cried Miss Tomasina.

So the Pilot did, stretching out a strong right arm to haul her up, while she in turn hauled up Algernon with Bernard hanging on to him, and in two shakes all were embarked.

'What day is it?' panted Miss Tomasina.

'Wednesday the nineteenth,' said the Pilot, 'or rather, since it's just past midnight, Thursday the twentieth.'

'Then it's my birthday!' cried Miss Tomasina. 'I may still be in time!'

As soon as she had explained all the circumstances, and how absolutely vital it was she should appear before the Court of Estates in person, the Pilot threw his schedule to the winds and headed the helicopter back for the city.

'What time does the Court sit?' he asked.

'At ten in the morning,' said Miss Tomasina. 'Please hurry!'

'We'll make it,' said the Pilot, 'with a lift from the landing-ground. But I doubt whether there'll be time for you to go anywhere first . . .'

'Why should I want to go anywhere first?' asked Miss Tomasina.

'Well, for an heiress to great estates,' said the Pilot, 'you do look a bit of a ragamuffin!'

It was true. Miss Tomasina hadn't seen herself in a mirror for weeks, and when she now did, in a pocket glass supplied by the Navigator, she cried out in dismay. Under the goatskin cap with its draggled ribbons her short hair hung in tangled elf-locks, and under the elf-locks showed a white pinched face so begrimed by dirt and tear stains, the identifying beauty spot was quite invisible . . .

'Take my handkerchief,' said the Pilot, 'and I think there's somewhere a bottle of tonic-water; and my Navigator, who's a bit of a dandy, usually carries not only a mirror but a comb.'

Though it reeked of Masculine Man Hair Lotion, Miss Tomasina was far from disdaining to use it—and only when her face was fairly clean, and her hair fairly in order,

did she suddenly realize she was wearing not only a greasy goatskin cap but greasy goatskin breeches!

'It's a pity we don't carry a Hostess,' said the Pilot. 'A Hostess would fix you up in no time!'

'Actually, though we haven't a Hostess on board, we've a Hostess's overall,' said the Navigator diffidently, 'that I borrowed to wipe down our windows with . . .'

'Severe reprimand and loss of pay,' said the Pilot. 'Is it still fairly clean?'

'I'm sure it's clean enough for *me* to wear!' cried Miss Tomasina, 'and please thank the Hostess very much!'

While all this was going on no one took much notice of Bernard and Algernon. In fact no one took any notice of them at all; Miss Tomasina had let go of Algernon (and so of Bernard too) when she reached for the Pilot's handkerchief, and though she thought of thanking the Hostess (who wasn't even there), quite forgot to thank her saviours. However she still wasn't altogether herself, and no wonder, so Bernard and Algernon bore no grudge, but made themselves as comfortable as they could in and on a box of Kleenex, also the property of the Navigator— Bernard by burrowing into its lower layers while Algernon settled down on top. Their prisoner-rescuing had succeeded indeed, but both were tireder than they had ever been in their lives!

'I'd still like to be there,' murmured Algernon, 'when the Court of Estates sits!'

'Don't worry,' said Bernard. 'The Pilot will be there— if you ask me he's a bit sweet on Miss Tomasina already!— and I've had a look at his greatcoat hanging up. In its pockets there'll be ample room for both of us!'

They flew on towards the clear, translucent dawn. Below them the bandits huddled in their cave, below *them* Rufus and Rusty and Ruby and Red curled close to their mother, as up the helicopter soared towards the brightening sky . . .

Or was there a hint of fog about?

12

FOG!

DAWN HAD SCARCELY dawned before the big chamber in the Parliament building was being cleaned up ready for the Court of Estates to sit—for it was so long since it last sat, all was festooned with cobwebs and deep in dust. Half-a-dozen scrubwomen were employed to sweep, and mop, and polish the windows, and among them Amy and Addie from the Young Ladies' Boarding School.

'My goodness!' said Amy. 'It's worse than the young ladies' dormitory!'

'At least no mice about!' said Addie.

'No, but spiders,' said Amy. 'And which are the worst I really don't know!'

'Nasty creepy-crawly things indeed!' agreed Addie. 'Touching your Easter bonnet with the pink rose on it, mightn't two think alike?'

'Not if one had the thought first,' said Amy.

'See what a whole nest of spiders I've brought down!' exclaimed Addie. 'Do sweep it into *your* sack, dear!'

'I've told you, I can't abear spiders any more than mice!' cried Amy. 'Sweep it into *yours*, dear—and we'll both have pink roses!'

'And you'll the pair of you have your noses put out of joint,' observed a third scrubwoman, overhearing, 'when you see me with not only roses but feathers, on *my* Easter bonnet!'

But however preoccupied with millinery, all did a very good job, and the chamber where the Court of Estates was to sit was left clean as a new pin.

'I just hope that horrid fog doesn't come creeping in!' said the third scrubwoman. 'I felt fog in the air when I got up!'

She should have been hired as a weather forecaster by the Air Ministry. However clear and translucent dawn had dawned, there was undoubtedly fog in the offing . . .

If the fog was approaching the city, it was already rolling in great waves down from the mountains above the Wolf Range—striking almost as swiftly as an avalanche, and to an aircraft quite as deadly!

'I'm very sorry, Miss Tomasina,' said the Pilot, 'but I think I'd better ground as soon as I see a flat area to land on.'

'No, no!' cried Miss Tomasina. 'If you do, we may be too late!'

'I happen to have several thousand pounds' worth of Government property in my charge,' pointed out the Pilot.

'My estate shall pay for all!' cried Miss Tomasina.

'Or we may all have our necks broken flying into an outlying spur of the Wolf Range . . .'

'If *I'll* take the risk, I'm sure you will too!' cried Miss Tomasina.

'Come on, Sir,' said the Navigator. 'Take a chance!'

(No one consulted Bernard and Algernon; though in fact both were ready to take a chance too.)

'Very well,' said the Pilot, 'but it'll be flying blind . . .'

'I can't say I like this case at all,' complained the Judge of the Court of Estates to his wife, as he finished breakfast and prepared to get into the striped trousers and morning coat he always wore under his robes. 'Miss Tomasina having

disappeared so very recently—and just before her eighteenth birthday!—I don't like this case at all . . .'

'You've only to do your duty as laid down by law,'
consoled his wife. 'What bothers *me*—you with your
bronchitis!—is all this fog about. You must take a muffler
and keep it over your nose.'

'And a pretty fool I should look,' said the Judge
irritably, 'under a wig *and* a muffler!'

'My word, that was a near shave!' exclaimed the Pilot.

Through the fog a spur of the Wolf Range had loomed
indeed, so close that the rotor was within feet of hitting it.
The helicopter bounced and lurched as he struggled at the
controls; Miss Tomasina and the Navigator hung on for
dear life to whatever strap or girder came to hand, and
Algernon was thrown completely off the box of Kleenex.
(Bernard, lower down, merely felt—if merely is the right
word—a sort of earthquake.) But as soon as they were on
an even keel again, all Miss Tomasina wanted to know
was what time it was.

'Ask the Navigator,' snapped the Pilot. 'I'm busy!'

'Eight-thirty-three,' said the Navigator.

'Then there's still time!' cried Miss Tomasina.

'Look out!' cried the Pilot. 'Here we go again!'

For scarcely had he dodged the first when a second spur
of the Wolf Range reared up, and having zigzagged once
the Pilot had to zigzag again. Fortunately he had uncommonly strong wrists, and the machine was in shipshape
order, otherwise all might have had their necks broken

indeed. As it was, Algernon bounced back onto the Kleenex box, and Bernard, peering up from its lower recesses,
asked him what on earth was going on.

'Fog!' replied Algernon. 'Fog's what's going on—but
how different from a London fog!' (Rather as a Victorian
Englishwoman, witnessing Sarah Bernhardt in the part of
Phèdre, had observed how different from their own dear
Queen.) 'I've never seen such a fog as *this* before!'

'Trust our Pilot,' said Bernard.

'Obviously there's nothing else to do,' said Algernon,
'except pray. Actually I once, when I was shut up in that
play-box, made a pretty good prayer. Shall I say it now?'

'I'd like to hear it,' said Bernard politely.

Algernon cleared his throat.

'O Lord of Bears, with golden coat,
  And boot-button eyes like stars,
Look down upon all Soft Stuffed Toys,
  And keep them in your charge.'

'It doesn't rhyme,' objected Bernard, who had been
schooled in verse by Miss Bianca. '*Stars* and *charge* don't
rhyme. A short prayer I myself happen to have composed,
does.'

'I'd like to hear it,' said Algernon, with equal politeness;
and Bernard cleared his throat in turn.

'O Lord of mice,
Save us from traps, and every other man's device.'

'Is that all?' asked Algernon.

'At least it rhymes,' said Bernard.

'Shall I tell you a prayer I made up,' murmured Miss
Tomasina to the Navigator—the Pilot was obviously too

busy struggling at the controls to listen—'while in cap-
tivity amongst the bandits?'

'I'd like to hear it,' said the Navigator.

'*O Lord above,*' murmured Miss Tomasina,
    Pity my plight!
Look down in compassion,
    And make everything right!'

'My prayer, when in a jam,' said the Navigator, 'goes
roughly,

    O Lord of the skies,
        Grant us Thy grace,
    Keep the engines going,
        And get us back to base.'

Obviously none of these prayers had any poetic merit,
but they were still heartfelt; and as Miss Tomasina and the
Navigator and Bernard and Algernon repeated them to
themselves, as suddenly as it had descended the fog began
to clear.

They might yet be in time!

13

THE END

IN A STATELY AND now clean room in the Parliament
House the Court of Estates was preparing to sit. It was an
impressive sight: on a high dais or platform presided the
Judge in scarlet robes and full-bottomed wig (but without
a muffler over his nose), with seated on either side of him
an Assessor in black robes and lesser wig, like a barrister's.
Before them, on the floor of the chamber, was a wide table
covered with green baize cloth, known as *La Table Verte*,
piled with title deeds and various other documents relating
to the property whose ownership they were about to assess
—and which Miss Tomasina's wicked guardian confidently expected to be assessed *his*!

The back part of the room was open to the public, and
was crowded with villagers and tenants—including the
wood-cutter whose gash Miss Tomasina had bound up
with her petticoat—who had come all the way from Three
Rivers in the hope, however faint, of seeing those
expectations disappointed; for all hated Miss Tomasina's
guardian from the bottom of their hearts, for his cruel
practices of eviction and forced labour and turning them
off their commons. Even Nicodemus was there (for he

could get about a good deal better than he'd let on to Bernard), in a really good place under the platform's ledge.

Miss Tomasina's guardian had chosen to appear in deep mourning, with a black-edged handkerchief which he frequently applied to his hypocritical old eyes—as green with greed and envy as the baize table-cloth! If the ploy bamboozled the Judge, it didn't bamboozle the tenants and villagers; as he stepped forward to take the oath, all booed and hissed like the geese on one of the commons he'd stolen from them!

'Silence in court!' ordered the Judge. 'Or the court shall be cleared!'

The booing and hissing subsided; Miss Tomasina's guardian, his oath taken, proceeded to express his belief that Miss Tomasina had not only been kidnapped by bandits, but also murdered by them—hence his mourning; then came to the point that as it was in any case her eighteenth birthday, and whether murdered or not she wasn't there to claim her inheritance, all fell rightfully into his hands.

'Certainly he has the law on his side,' murmured one of the Assessors.

'I fear he has,' said the Judge. 'Yet the fact that Miss Tomasina disappeared so very shortly before her eighteenth birthday rather troubles one.—Your ward having been missing scarcely a month,' he suggested, now addressing Miss Tomasina's guardian, 'might you not wait a little, before claiming her inheritance?'

'No,' said Miss Tomasina's guardian. 'Is the law the

law or isn't it? And is or isn't today her eighteenth birthday? It is; and unless she appears in person, all her heritage is legally mine. Unless she appears in person—'

'As I do!' cried Miss Tomasina, entering the court on the arm of the helicopter Pilot.

For within an hour of the fog's clearing he had regained his own landing ground, and though naturally all were surprised to see him back so soon, when he explained that he had the missing heiress on board, his superiors, instead of reprimanding him with loss of pay, laid on a fast car to take both of them to the Parliament House. But the Pilot had been quite right when he warned Miss Tomasina she wouldn't have time to go anywhere else first!

But even in the crumpled overall of an air hostess and with her hair cut short all the tenants and villagers recognized her at once—and what a scene of enthusiasm greeted her appearance!

''Tis Miss Tomasina!' cried one and all.

''Tis Miss Tomasina come back to us! Oh, what have they done to your pretty hair?' cried all the tenants' and villagers' wives. 'Oh, the villains, to take all your nice clothes away! But never mind, Miss Tomasina, we all know you for our rightful lady!'

'Silence in court!' cried the Judge. 'This changes the whole aspect of the case,' he added, aside to an Assessor.

Across the big green table Miss Tomasina's wicked guardian glared at her in fury—but so long as there was that barrier between them there was nothing else he could do. Miss Tomasina still clung rather hard to the Pilot's strong right arm, so that Bernard and Algernon, in his right-hand overcoat pocket were not only a good deal squeezed, but couldn't see a thing; but they could hear all right.

'So you, Miss Tomasina,' said the Judge, 'appearing here in court on your eighteenth birthday, claim, as you may, all rights to all estates and messuages bequeathed by your parents?'

'I do,' said Miss Tomasina boldly.

'Then the law awards them you,' judged the Judge, 'and the case is closed.'

'I protest!' cried Miss Tomasina's guardian. 'For how many years have I not protected her interests—'

'By turning us out of our homes and stealing our commons!' jeered all the villagers and tenants. 'If she hadn't been the sweetest young lady alive, you'd have made us hate *her* too!'

Miss Tomasina's wicked (now wretched) guardian staggered on his feet, and then in a fit of anger and apoplexy dropped down dead. To do him justice, he hadn't been quite wicked enough to attempt Miss Tomasina's life, but he'd bribed the pretended travelling showman to make off with her among the bandits, which was almost as bad.

'Let someone see the body carried out before we sit again,' said the Judge, withdrawing.

Immediately all the tenants and villagers swarmed about Miss Tomasina, saying how thankful they were to have her back, and out from under the ledge hobbled

Nicodemus on only one crutch, because he was waving the other in the air.

'What, are *you* here, Nicodemus?' exclaimed Miss Tomasina.

'Certainly I am,' said Nicodemus, 'and if it hadn't been for me you'd never have been rescued at all, for 'twas I who put your rescuers on the track!'

Which in a way was true, though it left out all Bernard's and Algernon's heroism.

'Then get into my pocket and come home with me to Three Rivers,' said Miss Tomasina, 'to live on cream cheese for the rest of your life!'

Which pressing invitation would at least get him out of Bernard's flat, and Bernard was so thankful he didn't mind having been, as he thought, once more forgotten. But Miss Tomasina, now entirely herself again, was a true lady.

'But where are the mouse and teddy bear who really rescued me?' she asked.

'By the feel of it,' said the Pilot, who'd just been groping there for a handkerchief, 'in my right-hand overcoat pocket . . .'

He hauled Bernard and Algernon out and set them absolutely on *La Table Verte*, and Miss Tomasina made them the most gracious speech possible.

'Dear friends,' said she, 'well I am aware how much I owe to you! Nicodemus may have put you on my track—'

'Indeed I did!' squeaked Nicodemus.

'—but 'twas your heroism that made my escape possible, and I thank you from the bottom of my heart. If you too

would care to come back with me to Three Rivers, you will be welcome indeed!'

Bernard, on the green baize cloth, took two steps back, then one forward, and pulled his whiskers, while Algernon bowed from where his waist used to be before he ate so much in the bandits' larder.

'Think nothing of it,' said Bernard, 'it was just a run-of-the-mill Prisoners' Aid operation.'

'Hear, hear,' said Algernon.

'And in fact, now we're home,' said Bernard, 'and

though we fully appreciate your kind offer, we'd rather
stay where we are—eh, Algernon?'

'Hear, hear,' repeated the bear.

'Not only heroic,' approved the Pilot, 'but dashed
sensible. Now I'll see *you* home, Miss Tomasina!'

Lovingly he looked into her eyes, lovingly she looked
into his—Bernard and Algernon forgotten again! The
Pilot and Miss Tomasina drifted dreamily out; the Court
room emptied, and Bernard and Algernon were left to
make the best way down they could from *La Table Verte*,
and then out and past the biggest house on the Grand
Boulevard—what memories it evoked in both their
breasts!—back to the Embassy and Miss Bianca's Porcelain
Pagoda.

It may have been noticed that Miss Bianca was not present
at the Court of Estates, even though she knew all about it
and what time it was to sit; and the reason for this was that
she was still completely ignorant of the success of
Bernard's prisoner-rescuing operation. So far as Miss
Bianca knew, Bernard was still somewhere in the Wolf
Range and Miss Tomasina as well; and she had no wish to
witness the triumph of the latter's wicked guardian. Had
she known the triumph was to be Bernard's, nothing
would have kept her from the Court—but as it was
Bernard was able to give her a glorious surprise when
he rushed into the Pagoda garden and told her all his
tale.

Miss Bianca's huge brown eyes grew even huger as she

listened with ever increasing admiration. At the bit about the wolf cubs, and Ruby's compassion, a tear stood in each, while at the blood-curdling bit about the bandits and their leader who wore an eye-patch with a cross on it, her whiskers trembled in sympathetic horror. The moment when Bernard recognized Miss Tomasina was thrilling indeed—Miss Bianca thrilled in every limb—and scarcely less so the moment when an aircraft of her own cherished helicopter flight swooped down in final rescue! Other exciting bits, such as their running into fog, Bernard left out, in case she quite fainted from too much emotion.

'So Miss Tomasina has been rescued indeed,' re-capped Miss Bianca at last, 'to appear in person at the Court of Estates and claim her inheritance from her wicked guardian?'

'Certainly she did,' said Bernard. 'And there'll be no more trouble from *him*, because he's dead as a doornail.—I'm sorry about your garden, Miss Bianca.'

'As if *that* mattered!' cried Miss Bianca. 'Oh, Bernard, how proud I am of you!'

'It was only a run-of-the-mill rescue,' said Bernard modestly, 'which since you weren't there I thought I'd better undertake myself . . .'

'But all alone,' exclaimed Miss Bianca, 'but for a soft toy!'

'Algernon?' said Bernard. 'Why, he proved as stout-hearted a companion as Nils! You haven't met him yet, Miss Bianca, but he's just outside.'

Algernon could no more get between the golden

palings surrounding Miss Bianca's garden than he'd been able to get into Bernard's flat, but as he now pressed his nose to them Miss Bianca extended a grateful hand and laid it caressingly on his muzzle.

'If it was you Bernard wanted to impress I don't wonder at his reckless resolution,' said Algernon. 'Really and truly—'

Here the bear suddenly paused, while a light of joy shone in his boot-button eyes.

'Did you hear what I just said?' he demanded excitedly. 'Bernard, Miss Bianca, did you hear what I just said? "Reckless resolution"! "Really and truly"!—Radishes, rhubarb and raspberries!' pronounced Algernon joyfully. 'Ravioli, rice pudding and roly-poly! Somewhere in the Wolf Range I've lost my lisp!'

So he had, though neither he nor Bernard had noticed, and exactly where is uncertain. In any case Bernard offered warm congratulations, adding that he for his part hadn't wanted to impress anyone, it was simply a matter of duty such as any Secretary of the M.P.A.S. would undertake, and it was Algernon's reckless resolution that deserved praise since he wasn't even a member.

'But where will you go now?' he added anxiously. 'Now that I've led you from the peace and security of a play-box in a Young Ladies' Boarding School?'

'Why, into the *Boy's* play-box,' said Miss Bianca. 'Or rather, into the extremely commodious bottom drawer where he keeps all the rest of his toys he's grown out of. There's at least one teddy bear there already to keep you company!'

'Does he come from London?' asked Algernon eagerly.

'Certainly,' said Miss Bianca. 'He was a gift from the British Ambassador.'

'Then we'll form a Club,' said Algernon, 'and call it the St. James's!'

(To look ahead a bit, so they did. It was the most exclusive club ever known, since Algernon and the other bear, whose name was Nigel, regularly black-balled any other soft toy who wanted to join. But each month they held a Ladies' Night, at which Miss Bianca, escorted by Bernard, was guest of honour.)

'It's going to be the very place for me,' decided Algernon happily. 'Just stroke my nose again, Miss Bianca, and I believe I'll have a nap till Bernard can take me round, for I'm really uncommonly exhausted!'

Was it exhaustion indeed, or was it tact, that led him immediately to sink into slumber curled up with his muzzle between his paws outside the Pagoda garden?

'Poor bear, how tired he is!' said Miss Bianca. 'And how tired you must be too, my dear, dear Bernard!'

'Just a bit whacked,' admitted Bernard. 'Did you miss me at all, Miss Bianca, while you were away at that mountain resort?'

'Did I miss you!' exclaimed Miss Bianca. 'You were hardly absent from my thoughts! I even wrote a poem about you!'

'Really?' cried Bernard. 'Really and truly? Oh Miss Bianca, won't you repeat it to me?'

''Twas but a *jeu d'esprit* which I've almost forgotten,' said Miss Bianca.

'Can't you remember even a line or two of it?' pressed Bernard.

'Well, the *last* two,' said Miss Bianca, 'were *O Bernard are you all right/Out of my sight?*'

Bernard drew a deep, happy breath.

'Of course I'm never *all right*, out of your sight,' said he, 'and I certainly wasn't all right in the Wolf Range among the bandits—'

'I know you haven't told me half,' said Miss Bianca, 'of the perils you underwent!'

'I'd undergo each and every one of 'em again, and twenty times over,' said Bernard, 'to earn even a syllable in one of your poems. To me, it's better than being in the M.P.A.S. Records Book.'

By the Venetian glass fountain their whiskers slightly yet thrillingly touched. But Miss Bianca was too wise to let the thrilling moment prolong itself.

'And now,' she said briskly, 'after you've woken up Algernon and introduced him to the bottom drawer, I expect you'll want to go round to your flat and evict that really deplorable Nicodemus!'

Starting from a dream of bliss—

'He's gone already,' said Bernard, 'in Miss Tomasina's pocket. But I suppose I'd better be there to put the laundry out.'

'Is it such a toil to you?' asked Miss Bianca sympathetic-ally.

'Well, a bit of a toil,' acknowledged Bernard. 'I always

seem to forget the whisker-towels until half-a-dozen have to go at once and there's nothing to dry my face on.'

Miss Bianca took a rapid decision.

'Dear Bernard,' said she, 'though we can never be more than best, best friends, why not come and live here in the Porcelain Pagoda, and *I'll* put your laundry out for you?'

Now it was Bernard who showed wisdom.

'No, Miss Bianca,' he said. 'If we can never be more than best, best friends, I'll go back to my flat in the cigar-cabinet (which really suits me very well), and just visit you as usual between five and seven every evening!'

Miss Tomasina almost immediately married the heli-copter Pilot, who gave up his career in the Air Force to help her look after her estates, which soon became the best and most humanely run of any in the country.—'One thing I'm determined on,' declared Miss Tomasina, 'is that none of my tenants shall ever pull their forelocks to me again—now that I know what it's like!'

She made in fact a far better proprietress than if she'd never been stolen by bandits, and her husband backed her up. On each anniversary of their wedding day all the villagers and tenants turned out with flags and bouquets— but not one ever pulled his forelock!

A Selected List of Fiction from Mammoth

While every effort is made to keep prices low, it is sometimes necessary to increase prices at short notice. Mandarin Paperbacks reserves the right to show new retail prices on covers which may differ from those previously advertised in the text or elsewhere.

The prices shown below were correct at the time of going to press.

☐	7497 0978 2	**Trial of Anna Cotman**	Vivien Alcock	£2.99
☐	7497 1510 3	**A Map of Nowhere**	Gillian Cross	£2.99
☐	7497 1066 7	**The Animals of Farthing Wood**	Colin Dann	£3.99
☐	7497 0914 6	**Follyfoot**	Monica Dickens	£2.99
☐	7497 0184 6	**The Summer House Loon**	Anne Fine	£2.99
☐	7497 0443 8	**Fast From the Gate**	Michael Hardcastle	£2.50
☐	7497 1784 X	**Listen to the Dark**	Maeve Henry	£2.99
☐	7497 0136 6	**I Am David**	Anne Holm	£3.50
☐	7497 1473 5	**Charmed Life**	Diana Wynne Jones	£3.50
☐	7497 1664 9	**Hiding Out**	Elizabeth Laird	£2.99
☐	7497 0791 7	**The Ghost of Thomas Kempe**	Penelope Lively	£2.99
☐	7497 0634 1	**Waiting for Anya**	Michael Morpurgo	£2.99
☐	7497 0831 X	**The Snow Spider**	Jenny Nimmo	£2.99
☐	7497 0412 8	**Voices of Danger**	Alick Rowe	£2.99
☐	7497 0410 1	**Space Demons**	Gillian Rubinstein	£2.99
☐	7497 0656 2	**Journey of 1000 Miles**	Ian Strachan	£2.99
☐	7497 0796 8	**Kingdom by the Sea**	Robert Westall	£2.99

All these books are available at your bookshop or newsagent, or can be ordered direct from the address below. Just tick the titles you want and fill in the form below.

Cash Sales Department, PO Box 5, Rushden, Northants NN10 6YX.
Fax: 0933 410321 : Phone 0933 410511.

Please send cheque, payable to 'Reed Book Services Ltd.', or postal order for purchase price quoted and allow the following for postage and packing:

£1.00 for the first book, 50p for the second; **FREE POSTAGE AND PACKING FOR THREE BOOKS OR MORE PER ORDER.**

NAME (Block letters) ....

ADDRESS ....

....

☐ I enclose my remittance for ....

☐ I wish to pay by Access/Visa Card Number

Expiry Date

Signature ....

Please quote our reference: MAND